Hannah

BRIDES OF THE OREGON TRAIL
BOOK ONE

CYNTHIA WOOLF

Published by Firehouse Publishing
Interior formatting: Author E.M.S.

Books written by Cynthia Woolf can be obtained either through the author's official website or through select, online book retailers.

www.cynthiawoolf.com

Books by Cynthia Woolf

CHAPTER 1

Independence, Missouri, May 1, 1852

Fifty-five wagons, with all their draft animals, cattle and goats, were in the staging area for the wagon train's start westward to Oregon City in Washington Territory. This wagon train was unlike any other that came before it. It was a train of mail-order brides. One-hundred and three women promised to miners, lumberjacks, and businessmen in Oregon City, population approximately nine-hundred-seventy-nine souls. All the women, except one, answered ads in the local newspaper put there by the men seeking wives.

The one who wasn't a bride was Hannah Granger.

Until very recently Hannah worked as a seamstress in a tailor shop. She lost her job after she slapped the store's owner for treating her like she was on the menu and he was the diner. Until the incident happened, she'd hoped she would learn enough from him to open her own dress shop one day. That dream still held her and she would just do it in Oregon City not Independence.

Her younger sister, Lydia, was a writer but her sales of articles to the newspaper weren't often enough to live off of. She hadn't sold a newspaper article in a month. Their rent was due today and without help they had enough to either pay the rent or eat. They'd been surviving this way since their parents died two years ago.

Until Mr. Walter Mosley came to their rescue. Out of desperation, Lydia had answered an ad for a mail-order bride more than a year ago and the man sent five hundred dollars to buy a wagon, a tent, and all the other supplies needed to cross the country to Oregon City where he lived.

Now Hannah helped her baby sister load the last of their belongings into the covered farm wagon. This wagon was fairly light, capable of carrying twenty-five hundred pounds and pulled by three yokes of oxen. The wagon had high clearance and was still sturdy enough to carry them over the mountains and through the rivers without getting stuck.

They'd packed up their apartment and been gone before the landlord came for the rent. They now slept in the wagon. By the time they started westward they would already be used to staying in the wagon at night.

She'd be glad to get away from Independence. All the wagons, with all the livestock and all their droppings made the staging area stink to high heaven. And she was getting used to it. She didn't like that at all.

More than half of Mr. Mosley's money went into buying the wagon and supplies they would need. They had packed flour, bacon packed in bran so the heat wouldn't melt the fat, coffee, baking soda, hardtack, jerky, dried beans, fruit, and beef, molasses, vinegar, pepper, four dozen eggs packed in cornmeal, salt, sugar, rice, tea, and lard. The staples would last for part of the long journey ahead. Along with the supplies, they bought two repeating rifles, with ammunition.

Their milk cow and two head of beef cattle would follow the wagon until the time came to slaughter one of the beef cows to provide meat to be shared by everyone on the wagon train. With more than one-hundred-fifty people, the meat was used quickly.

Mr. Titus—the man they'd hired to help outfit them, teach them to drive a team of six oxen and to shoot a rifle—was a fount of information.

"You ladies can hang the milk bucket under the wagon and let the wagon's movements churn the milk into butter. You can have fresh butter every day which is good when you're down to just beans and biscuits. And don't think you won't get there. Everyone gets to that point."

He was probably in his sixties, with silver-white hair and a well-trimmed beard he pulled to a point on his chin when he was frustrated. He'd been to Oregon and back on a wagon train every year between 1846 and 1850. He knew exactly what to take and what to leave. Plus, he'd been outfitting emigrates with wagons and supply lists for the last two years.

This wagon train was unusual. With very few exceptions everyone on the train was a mail-order bride, including her sister Lydia.

Lydia was a pretty girl, much prettier than she was, thought Hannah. Lydie had long golden blonde hair, blue eyes, and a figure that put most other women to shame. But at twenty-one she was an old maid. Hannah supposed she was too, at twenty-three. In any case, neither of them had found men she wanted to marry. Lydia figured, if she was to marry just to be married, she might as well marry the rich, old man, who'd seemed nice in his letter.

Mr. Walter Mosley had been upfront in his first correspondence. He told her he was sixty-one and hit it rich in the California gold fields before moving to Oregon City. He promised to provide for her and any family she wanted to bring.

Hannah heard yowling and came around the corner of the wagon where she saw Lydie with a tiny three-legged kitten. Hannah shook her head. *Here we go again. She's collecting strays already and we haven't even left town yet.*

"Lydia, what are you doing with that cat?"

Lydie pulled the kitten to her side, like she was protecting him from Hannah. "I found him in the alley. The mercantile owner would have killed him if I hadn't stepped in. He's just a baby, probably not more than four or five weeks old, if that."

The little thing really was making an awful racket. Hannah wasn't surprised the store owner wanted to destroy it, but still, the animal was just a baby, probably missing its mama.

She sighed and shook her head…now they had a pet. Hannah wondered how many more strays Lydie would pick up before the trip was over.

"I have to admit, he's awfully cute and with just three legs he wouldn't last long alone. You're a good woman, Lydie."

The kitten was so little, mostly gray with black feet and he had the sweetest face with the greenest eyes she'd ever seen. Greener even than Hannah's own.

"I need to bathe him. He's mangy and full of fleas. I'm not putting him in the wagon this way." Lydia grabbed her lavender soap and walked over to the horse trough and gave him a bath, which he didn't like at all. Then she carried him back to the wagon by the scruff of his neck and dried him off. Turned out he was really dirty. By the time his bath was finished, he was white with dark gray feet.

Lydie fed him cornmeal mixed with a raw egg. After the cat licked the plate clean, he seemed happier. When Lydie picked him up and cuddled him in her arms, he didn't protest like before but settled in and began to purr. As always, Lydie had made a friend of a wounded animal.

They'd packed all their clothes, which weren't many, but they left the hoops behind and raised the hems of their skirts. The hoops might be fashionable, but they would just get in the way on this journey. She and Lydie needed to be free to move around, get on and off the wagon and probably walk for hours beside the six oxen pulling their wagon.

They chose oxen to pull the wagon because Mr. Titus said they ate rougher grass and didn't need much in the way of grain, so less to haul. The animals were stronger than a horse or a mule should the wagon need to be pulled out of a problem of some kind or another, which Hannah was sure they'd need before the trip was over.

She walked to the front of the wagon where Mr. Titus stood.

"Are you ladies sure you're prepared for this trip?" Concern etched his wrinkled features.

"Yes, sir," answered Hannah as she again checked the tie downs on the wagon cover. "As prepared as we'll ever be. I'm sure we'll learn a lot over the course of the next five or six months."

He walked over to her and handed her a small burlap bag. "You will. Here is an extra pound of coffee. You'll need it."

She looked from the bag to the man and then hugged him. "Thank you, Mr. Titus. We really appreciate this."

Beet red, he waved off her thanks. "You girls… err…ladies, have a tough road ahead. Whenever you get a chance to rest, take it. At times you won't get to stop for more than a few hours because you need to be over the mountains as soon as possible. You may have to travel in the dark when the weather is nice enough. Riding in the wagon is terribly hard on the body. Unless you're driving the team, I recommend you walk.

If Mr. Titus had been trying to scare her, it worked. Hannah didn't want to go, but she had no choice either. They had no money and had spent three hundred of the five hundred dollars. All she and Lydia had was each other and soon Mr. Mosley would be part of their little family.

Hannah wasn't sure Lydia was making the best decision when it came to marrying Mr. Mosley even though he was wealthy. He was old, but Lydia said he sounded nice in his letter.

Their wagon master was Chester Gunn, an older man, probably in his forties, with graying brown hair, a gray mustache, and nice brown eyes. He was not particularly tall, just a few inches more than her own five-foot-seven-inch height, but he was slender and wiry looking. His mere presence invited trust.

"You ladies packed up?" he asked while perched atop his gray stallion. "The front of the train has already started. We'll get to you in about half an hour, then we won't stop until we make camp at dusk. There's a little creek we pull alongside where you can get water for cooking and not have to use that in your barrel. Are you ready to go?"

Hannah nodded. "Yes, sir. We're more than ready."

Gunn smiled. "Good. That's what I like to hear."

"Um, Mr. Gunn. Have you ever had a wagon train full of brides before?" Lydia held the little cat, stroking him and he purred in her arms.

"No, Miss Granger. A wagon train with more than one-hundred women is a first for me. That's why I had to hire the extra men." He pointed at the man with him. "This here is Dick Bailey, he's one of our outriders."

"Pleased to meet you, Mr Bailey."

The slender man with blonde hair hanging loose, tipped his hat. "The pleasure is mine, Miss Granger."

Chester continued. "Our journey will be a rough one and you and the rest of the ladies will be tested like you never have before. If you want to back out, now is the time, not after we get underway because I can't send any of the men to return with you. You'd be on your own."

Lydia vigorously shook her head. "Oh, no, sir. We don't want to back out. I was just curious, that's all. I have a man waiting on the other end. We're definitely not backing out."

Mr. Gunn smiled. "Good. You two have gumption. You're going to need it."

He tipped his hat and rode on to the next wagon.

Hannah and Lydia were about in the middle of the fifty-five wagon train, a fact for which Hannah was glad. The closer to the front, the easier the trip would be. At least that's what she thought. Bringing up the rear would mean eating everyone else's dust and she figured she and Lydia would have plenty of dirt kicked up by the animals and wagons in front of them.

"Time to put the kitten in the wagon and climb up, Lydia."

She nodded and placed the kitten just inside the bed of the wagon where she had taken a couple of towels and made a little bed for him.

Hannah watched shook her head and rolled her eyes. She knew Lydia couldn't turn away any animal in need and wondered how many hurt or abandoned creatures they'd have with them by the time they reached Oregon City.

The wagon train was slow moving. The oxen walked. They didn't trot or run...just a slow easy walk. That was the only way the animals would make it the two thousand miles to Oregon Country.

The food they'd laid in would have to last them until they reached Fort Laramie in the Nebraska Territory, which would put about one third of the journey behind them. They would have to conserve the two hundred dollars they had left, an amount equal to a year's earning for Hannah. No wonder people sold everything not nailed down to get enough money for the journey. As for them, though Mr. Mosley was very generous, they still had to be cautious. That money would have to buy their food, cover wagon repairs, medicine, if needed and perhaps even replace an ox.

They stopped next to Little Blue River at about dusk and, even though they traveled only about fifteen miles from Independence, Hannah was exhausted. She'd walked for hours today, as had Lydia and both were definitely the worse for wear. Hannah wanted to just lay down on the ground and go to sleep, but chores awaited, supper needed fixed and then dishes needed washed.

On top of that, Hannah's feet were killing her. She'd bought a new pair of boots for the journey, and they didn't fit as well as perhaps they should. She couldn't wait to go to the stream and cool her feet in the water.

After the wagons formed a corral, everyone unpacked their cooking and eating utensils for the evening meal. The oxen and cattle were allowed to graze during the night, just outside the circle of wagons, as long as Indians weren't around. Not that the travelers feared attack, but the Shoshone weren't above pilfering a cow or two.

Because of the Shoshone, Lydia and Hannah kept the milk cow tied with a rope to the back of wagon. They also put on her bell at night, so they'd know if anyone tried to steal her. The animal could still graze but was close enough to bring in quickly, if needed.

Hannah took care of the animals and making up their bed for the night. She and Lydia slept under the wagon as it was dry out. Rearranging the wagon so they could sleep in there took a long time and was a lot of work. While they waited for the wagon train to depart, they had slept in the wagon on the sacks of food rather than put them outside. Sleeping on them was as uncomfortable as sleeping on the ground.

Lydia prepared their supper of bacon, eggs, biscuits, and coffee. It didn't sound like much, but she made enough to fill up of each of them and together they finished every last morsel.

Lydia, of course, shared her bacon and eggs with the kitten. Hannah even saved a bit of her eggs for him. The little thing would be huge by the time they reached Oregon if he kept eating like this. But he never seemed to get full. Hannah thought maybe he was afraid he wouldn't be fed again so he begged from both of them until they relented and gave him a little more.

Hannah helped Lydia with the dishes and then fell into bed with her clothes on, too exhausted to go to the river and cool her feet. Even though she missed her soft bed, right now the pallet felt like heaven.

Morning came early and Mr. Gunn wanted to be back on the road by seven o'clock. Normally, she wouldn't be rising from bed until seven so she could be to work by eight. This new reality would take a while to become routine.

A bugle sounded, followed by a shotgun blast. Hannah sat upright and hurried out of the covers, peering through the wagon wheel to see what was happening. Then she realized it was dawn and this was how they would be awakened.

She wet a washcloth from the water bucket. They'd used the water from the barrel, too tired to go to the river and fill the bucket. Hannah knew she'd have to fill the barrel back up and start using the river water but for now she washed her face and hands. Now would have been a good time to take care of her feet, but she had to care for the animals first. By the time she was done with that, Lydia would have breakfast ready and then they'd have to repack to be ready to get back on the trail by seven.

Oh, well. I'll do it tonight. The day will be a rough one. They already hurt. It's my own fault for waiting so long to buy the boots. If I'd purchased them sooner, I

"I intend on joining it myself. I understand Chester Gunn is looking for extra men to ride along."

"I wouldn't know, but that would make sense. Most of us are mail-order brides. There are about one hundred women in fifty wagons. Don't you need a horse in order to ride along?"

"He's over there grazing about fifty feet from here. I'm surprised you didn't hear me. That's not a good survival instinct."

"I was concentrating on other things."

Mr. Stanton pointed at her feet. "Walking on those feet will hurt like hell. You should ride in the wagon until they heal."

Tears in her eyes from the pain, she pulled off the sock. "Oh, God." She looked up at the man in front of her. "Riding in the wagon is almost as bad as trying to walk on these feet. Besides, I don't have any choice, Mr. Stanton. I can't let my sister walk all the time. And I can't let her know about this." *Lydia would be compassionate, but she'd scold me. Being scolded by your little sister is embarrassing.*

"All right. I'll keep your secret. Let me help you now."

"How?"

"I'll carry you to the stream. Standing in the cool water will help your feet feel better and clean the wounds at the same time."

Hannah looked at him again. He wore a chambray shirt with the sleeves rolled up to the elbow and black wool pants. She still couldn't see much of his face. His jaw was covered with several days growth of beard and he sported a well-groomed moustache over perfect lips. He didn't seem to want to harm her; he could have done that without ever letting her know of his presence.

"Thank you. I'd appreciate that. I need to wash out those socks, too."

He held out his hand. "Can you stand?"

"Yes, I think so." She picked up the bloody socks, took his hand and stood on the grass surrounding the rock.

Joe scooped her into his arms and carried her to the stream.

To her surprise, he didn't set her down on the bank but carried her right into the water before letting her down carefully in the shallows.

"How's that feel?"

Hannah sighed. "Wonderful. If the water wasn't so cold that my feet would freeze solid, I'd stand here all night. As it is, I better get these socks washed and then get back to camp." She needed to thank him somehow. "Would you care to join my sister and me for supper, Mr. Stanton?"

"Only if you call me, Joe."

"All right, Joe. Call me Hannah. I figure we're headed to a new, young land and old etiquette doesn't matter. Let me get on my boots and you can walk back with me."

"You're mighty trusting for a young lady alone with a strange man."

She looked up, way up, at him. He had to be six two or six three by her estimation. He wasn't threatening like her former employer. He didn't leer at her or make her feel uncomfortable. Just the opposite. He was kind and gentle with her. Caring that she was in pain. She bet if she asked, he'd carry her all the way back to camp. Not that she'd ask, of course. "If you were going to harm me, you wouldn't have warned me of your presence by speaking. You'd have just come up behind me and killed me. Besides, you helped me with my feet. I appreciate that."

"Let's keep as much dirt and mud out of your injuries as possible."

He scooped her into his arms again and carried her back to the rock, setting her down on it.

"Now, let me see if I can wrap those bandages around your feet." He pointed at the ground where her dry socks and the bandages sat. "Then you can put your socks on and hopefully feel better."

He was very careful and gentle while he dried her feet, applied the salve and wound the long strips of cloth around her feet and up her calf, tying a knot snugly at the top. Then he helped her don her socks and made her put each foot on his thigh so he could tie her boots. After which, he stood and extended his hand.

"Shall we see how good my doctorin' is?"

Hannah put both feet on the ground and tenderly stood. Her feet still hurt but it was tolerable now.

"You did great. I can actually walk with a minimum amount of pain. Come with me and we'll have supper."

Joe gathered his big, black horse and followed her back to camp. He tied the animal to the front of the wagon and then they went around the back into the wagon corral.

"Lydia, this is Joe Stanton. He...uh...helped me with the animals and I invited him to supper as a thank you."

Lydia smiled that smile of hers that had men smitten immediately.

She held out her hand. "Welcome, Mr. Stanton. I'm afraid all we have to offer is beef stew, biscuits, and coffee, but there's plenty. We'd be delighted if you'd join us."

He wiped his hands on his pants and then took hers. "Don't mind if I do. I'm mighty tired of hardtack and jerky."

"Come, sit by the fire. I've got supper about ready. Just waiting on the biscuits." Lydia poured him a cup of coffee. "Here you go."

"Thank you, ma'am. I'm much obliged."

Joe sat on one of the empty buckets they used as stools and sipped the hot coffee. Then he took off his hat.

Hannah sucked in a breath. The man was a god, handsome as all get out. Coal black hair that brushed his collar, dark blue eyes, tanned skin, and a square jaw.

"Hannah? Hannah?" Lydia snapped her fingers.

Startled and embarrassed to be caught staring, Hannah felt heat in her cheeks that was more than just the warmth of the fire.

"I'm sorry. What did you need?"

"Will you get Trinity? He needs to eat, too." Lydia took the Dutch oven off the fire and set it aside. Then she dished up a plate for Joe.

"Trinity?" asked Hannah.

"The kitten."

Hannah lifted an eyebrow. "When did you name it Trinity?"

"Today." Lydia removed the biscuits from the pot and placed them on a tin plate. "I thought it appropriate, since he only has three legs."

Joe spat out his coffee and burst into laughter.

"You have a three-legged cat?"

Lydia's mouth turned down and her eyebrows furrowed but then she chuckled and nodded. "Oh, yes. I rescued him from a man who was about to kill him. He's just a bitty thing, not even six weeks old. Hannah, please get him while I dish up our plates."

"Okay."

She went over to the wagon and called for the kitten, which meowed loudly. "Trinity. Kitten. Come here."

The cat bounded over the sacks of food to the back of the wagon and into Hannah's arms.

"There you go." She petted him while she walked back to the fire.

She leaned down and introduced Joe to the kitten.

"Joe, this is Trinity."

He reached up and scratched under Trinity's chin. "Hello there, little cat."

"Why Joe Stanton, you old bounty hunter, what are you doing on my wagon train? Hope you aren't bothering these nice ladies."

Hannah looked down at Joe. *A bounty hunter. I've never met a bounty hunter before. That's kind of like a lawman.*

She turned toward Mr. Gunn who approached from across the corral.

"Oh, no, Mr. Gunn. Joe's been very helpful to us. We thought to repay him with a meal."

Joe stood, set his plate on the bucket and greeted Mr. Gunn with a handshake. "You're looking good Chester. How is Clarice?"

A shadow fell over Chester's face. "She passed on last winter. Caught the flu and couldn't recover."

Joe's mouth turned down and clapped the man on the shoulder. "I'm sorry. She was a wonderful woman."

"That she was. I took on this one last wagon train for her. She was always tryin' to be a matchmaker and a wagon train full of mail-order brides bound for Oregon City would have pleased her. She might even have come on this one." Mr. Gunn narrowed his eyes. "She never had any luck with you, though."

"I'm not the marryin' kind anymore, Chester. You know that. What I do for a living doesn't go well with married life. I won't put another woman in that situation."

Mr. Gunn clapped Joe on the shoulder. "I know how you feel. But Sandra was never meant for this land. She turned into an Eastern lady through and through."

Joe stood one hand in his pocket the other at his side. "I thought we could get through anything. I was wrong. I won't go through that again."

"You could always be a wagon master."

"I couldn't ask that of a woman. To constantly be traveling, to never have a real home." He dropped his chin and looked at Chester. "Any more than you could have asked it of Clarice." He shook his head. "Nah, I don't have the temperament for this kind of work. I'll stick to being a scout, which I hear you're looking for. I'd like to apply for the job."

Chester grinned. "You want the job, you got it. Doesn't pay much, but you'll be fed three squares a day. Cookie's here with the chuck wagon and, as you can see, most of the ladies don't mind having an extra mouth or two at their meals."

"That's right." Hannah had heard more than enough. She handed Joe his plate. "We'd love to have the company. Speaking of which, Mr. Gunn, would you like to join us?"

Mr. Gunn waved off her request. "No, thank you. The ladies in the Bond wagon have already invited me."

Hannah set Trinity on the ground, picked up her plate and cup and then sat across the fire from Joe. She wanted to look at him. After she sat she decided gazing at him wasn't such a good idea. She found herself staring and quickly looked down at her plate. She was thinking about moving when a change in the wind made it impossible to continue sitting where she was.

Taking her plate and setting it on the ground next to Joe, she then got the bucket. "I hope you don't mind. The smoke has chased me from the other side."

"Not at all." He looked to his right, at Lydia and then back to Hannah. "I like being surrounded by beautiful women."

"You have a way with words, Joe. I almost believe you." Hannah sat and picked up her plate remembering all the men who'd only used her to get to Lydia. For some reason, she didn't have much of an appetite, but she ate anyway. Wasting good food was a bad thing and not to be done. As a compromise, she fed the cat.

"Trinity. Come here kitty."

The kitten, having figured out that when he responded to his name he usually got food, trotted over. He was very good at moving around with only three legs. He was missing the right front leg, but didn't seem to notice. Maybe because he was so young and learned to walk without it to begin with.

She put some of her eggs and bacon on the ground. "We really ought to designate one of the plates for his food. He can't continue to eat from our fingers and I worry he'll get too much dirt in his system if we keep putting it on the ground."

Lydia stood. "You're right. Let me get another tin plate. We have six after all."

She went to the box tied to the side of the wagon where all the cooking and eating utensils were kept, rummaged around and came back with a plate. Then she put on fresh food and placed it on the ground next to her. "Trinity. Come, kitten."

Trinity practically pounced on the plate, wolfing down the morsels of food.

Joe chuckled. "He's a hungry little thing, isn't he?"

Hannah laughed. "I hope he realizes he'll be fed on a regular basis fairly soon or he'll be fat in no time. He'll be hard-pressed to get around on those legs of his if he gains too much weight."

"He's fine," protested Lydia. "Once he gets used to us and to eating, he'll calm down."

"So, Joe, did I hear correctly, you're a bounty hunter as well as a scout? Isn't bounty hunting a fairly dangerous occupation?" asked Hannah, still in awe of meeting a real bounty hunter.

"No more dangerous than being a sheriff nowadays, and a heck of a lot more profitable." He took a sip of his coffee. "I figure I'm doing the country a service."

"Oh," Lydia put her nearly empty plate down and the cat ran to finish the food on the dish. "How's that? Your service to the country, I mean?"

"I get bad men off the street and behind bars or at the end of a rope, depending on what they've done," replied Joe.

"Have you ever brought in someone who was innocent?" asked Hannah. She watched as something passed in his dark eyes.

Shaking his head he sighed. "I thought one of my bounties was an innocent man. I was sure the story he told me was true and would be corroborated during the trial. I was wrong. He was guilty of the murder of a banker's wife. But as it turned out, the banker had hired the man to do it and then put up the reward so the man would be sure to hang. The man pleaded guilty hoping to avoid the hangman's noose, but he also implicated the banker who then shot the murderer and was then tried for murder. So the banker was stupid for putting up the bounty."

"Oh, my God." Hannah's hand flew to her throat. "He hired someone to kill his wife...but couldn't they have divorced instead of murder?"

"I don't know. You would have thought so. Anyway I don't get to know the person I'm collecting the bounty on anymore. As a matter of fact, the less I know the better. Besides, I guess in one way or another they're all guilty. Everyone is of something."

Hannah cocked her head to the side. "That's an awful cynical attitude."

He shrugged. "So far, I'm right. No one has proved me wrong yet."

"There's always a first time."

Joe watched the change in Hannah's face as she was saddened by his story. He wished he'd been able to tell her he'd never brought in an innocent man. Never thought that one of the men he captured was innocent. But he wouldn't lie.

For some reason, he couldn't lie to her and knew it was important that he not try.

"So, both of you ladies are mail-order brides, huh?" He finished the food on his plate and glanced between the sisters. They couldn't have looked more different. He thought most men would probably prefer Lydia with her blonde, blue-eyed, slender good looks. But he could hardly take his eyes off of Hannah. She had the cutest freckles across her nose and curly flame-red hair that was escaping the bun at her neck. And she had a very womanly figure which he liked. He wanted a woman who looked and felt like a woman, not a girl. Lydia was a girl compared to Hannah.

Hannah shook her head and waved her hand toward her sister. "Just Lydia."

Joe didn't understand why that knowledge pleased him, but it did.

"What are you planning to do in the Oregon Country?" he asked Hannah.

"Well, I'll be staying with Lydia, at least until I marry. I'm a seamstress by trade. Until just before we left, I worked for a tailor. I hope to open a dress shop when we get there. I've always dreamed of having my own shop. I'm hoping Mr. Mosley will help get me started. Meaning loan me the money to buy everything I need, material, thread, needles, everything. What I have with me won't make more than a dress for Lydie and me."

"Did you leave your job so you could come on this trip with your sister?"

Hannah stopped smiling and looked into the fire. "I left because the owner decided I wasn't just an employee, but his own plaything." She looked up at Joe. "I'm not any man's plaything."

"I would hope not."

He saw the blush creep into her face.

"Thank you. A lot of men wouldn't understand."

At that moment Trinity began to climb her skirt.

"No, Trinity. You'll ruin my dress with those sharp claws."

"He just wants to cuddle now that he's fed," called Lydia from the wagon where she was doing the dishes. "Put him in your lap."

Hannah shook her head and plucked the cat off her dress, settling him in her lap. "I know how to handle a kitten, I simply don't want him climbing my skirt. The sooner he learns that the better."

No sooner had she removed her hand than he walked in circles around her lap, looking for the best place before he lay down, though there wasn't much choice on her lap, he still had to do the ritual of finding the perfect spot to light. She was surprised that as young as he was he'd learned this behavior.

Once he was settled, he started to groom himself.

Hannah petted him, down his head and over his back to the end of his tail.

He purred.

"Looks like he's very content," said Joe. "So would I be, if I were in his place."

Hannah raised her eyebrows and her mouth formed an -O-. "You are a scoundrel, Joe Stanton," she said with a smile.

He raised his hands and grinned. "Guilty as charged. I should get on out of here. I still need to talk to Chester about some things."

He stood and looked from Hannah to Lydia and back again.

"Thank you, ladies, for a wonderful supper. I truly appreciate the home cooking."

Hannah picked up Trinity and stood. "I hope you'll come back again. We'd love to have you."

He donned his hat, throwing his eyes back into shadow.

"You can count on it."

He turned toward Lydia and tipped his hat.

"Good night, Miss Lydia."

"Good night, Joe."

He turned to Hannah, reached over and scratched Trinity behind the ears.

"Good night, Hannah."

"'night, Joe. See you tomorrow?"

"You bet." *You'll be seeing a lot of me Miss Hannah Granger.*

Hannah's heart hammered in her chest and her stomach did somersaults as she watched the tall man walk away. Sauntered was more like it. A bounty hunter. She'd never known anyone with a dangerous occupation, and she realized he was a danger to her, as well. She could easily lose her heart to such a man.

What would tomorrow bring?

Whatever it was, as long as Joe Stanton was in the picture, she was sure she'd have a great day.

CHAPTER 3

The following couple of weeks Hannah watched for Joe, but he always seemed busy when she came around.

She and Lydia both rode in the wagon today. Rain fell yesterday and was still coming down today. The trail was muddy and it was difficult to stay out of the ruts from other wagon trains. Hannah's boots made sucking sounds with every step. When Lydia suggested she ride beside her, she'd gladly agreed. Her feet were killing her. She needed to treat them again but didn't know if they would still be following the Little Blue River tomorrow.

Lydia found their slickers and they wore them, but the rain beat down mercilessly, soaking them anyway. Their bonnets, made from sturdy cotton, were wet and dripping water into their laps.

Hannah wanted more than anything to get in back with Trinity and wrap herself in a blanket but that wouldn't be fair to Lydia. Someone had to drive and getting the blankets soaked wasn't an option.

They stopped for the midday meal. Hannah's job was to care for the livestock, which also ate when they stopped. She watered them, found a good patch of grass for them to graze, tied each to a tree and then went back to the wagon.

Lydia sat in the back with a cup of water and hard tack.

"This is what we get for dinner today. No way I'm trying to start a fire in this weather."

Hannah climbed in beside her still wearing her rain slicker, though she felt like her clothes were wet and sticking to her body anyway. She'd probably catch her death of pneumonia. "I don't blame you. Hand me a piece of that, please."

Lydia reached into the sack with the food and brought out two pieces of the simple hard biscuit made from flour, water, and salt.

Hannah looked at the piece of dry bread. It would sustain life and keep her stomach from growling, but that's about all. Regardless of how it tasted, or more accurately, didn't taste, it would keep her going for now. She just hoped they didn't have to eat it for supper, too.

A knock sounded from the end of the wagon.

"You ladies all right?"

Joe.

Hannah's heart thumped wildly in her chest and her mouth went dry. A reaction to seeing Joe, not eating the dry biscuit.

"We're fine, Joe. What about you? Want to come in out of the rain for a bit?" asked Lydia.

"I'd love to. I'll be right back."

He was gone for a few minutes and then returned, climbing in through the front of the wagon.

Joe sat on a barrel, across the wagon from Hannah and Lydia, then took off his wet hat and placed it next to him.

Hannah wondered if he could hear her heart beat its rapid tattoo. For once, she was glad for the rain as it would disguise the clamminess of her hands.

"Sorry we can't offer you hot coffee, but it's a bit difficult to build a fire in this weather." Lydia jutted her chin toward the front opening.

"That's all right. It would have just gotten cold anyway."

Hannah reached into the bag of hard tack.

"Care for a biscuit?"

"Please." Joe took the food, his fingers brushing hers.

Sucking in a breath at the sudden shock of awareness she felt, Hannah glanced up at Joe. His eyes were wide and he seemed surprised.

Lydia was oblivious to what was happening between Joe and Hannah, their stillness. "We also

31

have some dried apples. I'm sorry we don't have anything else to offer for the meal."

"Not to worry. Perhaps I can add to our repast."

Joe reached inside his slicker and pulled out a small burlap bag from which he produced several pieces of dried meat.

"What kind of jerky is that?" asked Hannah, peering at the offering in his hand.

"This is elk meat. Got it from an Indian friend of mine. Try some. You have to chew it for a long time but luckily, it also has a good long lasting flavor."

He handed each of them a piece of meat.

Joe put it in his mouth and tore off a piece.

Hannah and Lydia did the same. He was right, the flavor was great, but it definitely took a while to make the 'jerky' able to swallow.

Lydia petted Trinity and the little cat sat contentedly purring on her lap. "So tell us how you became a bounty hunter. You won't be able to go outside for a while anyway."

"Oh, yes, please," said Hannah. She pulled her knees up to her chest and wrapped her arms around them, careful not to show any leg. "We've never known anyone with an occupation like yours. It must be so exciting."

Joe shrugged. "I don't know how exciting it is. I spend long days in the saddle tracking a fugitive. When I finally find him, I'm so tired of chasing him; I have little empathy for his plight and just tie him up and take him in. Not really very exciting."

"Oh, but you must see some beautiful country," persisted Hannah, unwilling to accept that his job was the least bit mundane. *I know from the adventure novels I've read there are beautiful places in the world. Surely Joe has seen some of them.*

Joe nodded. "That's true and the best part of doing what I do. I've seen mountains so high the clouds obscure the top, valleys so green and lush they take your breath away, and waterfalls that are thousands of feet high."

"The country sounds so beautiful," said Hannah, closed her eyes picturing the spectacular visions in her mind. "So far we've seen the prairie and the river. They are nice, but not spectacular by any means. No buildings to be seen and no people except for ourselves. This is very strange to me. Lydie and I grew up in Independence, with brick buildings, lots of shops, restaurants, banks, offices and, of course, homes. There is nothing out here. It's green, but empty."

"Be glad it's still green. We'll get to prairie that is dry as dust and brown without a drop of water in sight."

She opened her eyes. "Yes, I suppose we will. Joe, are there lady bounty hunters?"

He thought for a moment. "I suppose there are. I've never met one myself."

Hannah smiled and would have jumped up and down if it would help her get what she wanted. "Could you teach me to be a bounty hunter?"

Frowning Joe shook his head. "You're much too fragile for such a job. Besides you know nothing about the country, the Indians, the languages spoken...doing what I do would be very difficult for you."

"I'm not fragile and I'm a good pupil, I promise." *Being a seamstress is fun, but not exciting. I'd like to have some adventure in my life...as long as Joe's there, too.*

Lydia frowned at Hannah. "What's gotten into you? What about your dress shop. Is that no longer your dream? Instead you'd rather have the kind of lonely life Joe has described?"

Again he shook his head. "It's not a good idea, Hannah. My job, as you've just heard, is not glamorous. It's hard and tiring. You go without eating or sleeping in a soft bed. Your horse, in my case, Midnight, becomes your best friend. You don't want that. No one in their right mind does."

She glowered at both Lydia and Joe. "Aren't you in your right mind?"

"Maybe. Maybe I'm the exception to the rule."

"Oh, you're an exception, all right," said Hannah, under her breath.

Joe cocked an eyebrow. "What's that you said?"

"Nothing." She occupied herself with picking non-existent lint off her skirt.

Trinity woke up, stretched and wandered over to Joe, meowed at him and then lay in his lap.

"He likes you," commented Lydia.

Joe scratched the tiny feline behind the ears and around his head. "I have a way with animals. They usually like me."

"Well, he certainly does," said Lydia.

Joe glanced out the front opening and picked up his hat.

"Looks like the rain is stopping. I should probably get going."

Hannah wanted more than anything for him to stay but that was a desire she'd keep to herself.

"I suppose so. We should probably check on the animals as well. Do you think we'll travel anymore today?"

He shrugged, handed the kitten to Lydia, and then stood. "I don't know what Chester will decide to do. If it were me, I'd just stay here and then start fresh in the morning. But he might want to make some distance. The journey's long and even though we've been making good time, if we stay here; all the time we gained will be gone."

Hannah glanced out and saw the sun beginning to peek through the clouds. "Well, before we unpack the supper things, we'll wait and see what Mr. Gunn says."

"Good plan. Thank you, ladies, for the shelter, food and good conversation." He looked down at Hannah. "That's another downfall of my occupation. It's lonely with no one to talk to for days, sometimes weeks."

Hannah frowned. "Yes, not talking to anyone

would be bad. I like to talk as you probably have noticed."

His lip curled up a little and his eyes twinkled. "I had an inkling."

He stepped up on the wagon seat and then climbed down.

Hannah waved at his retreating form. "Goodbye, Joe."

Joe stopped, turned and waved his arm before mounting his horse.

She sat on the sacks of flour and sighed.

Lydia chuckled. Trinity had returned to her lap now that Joe was gone, and she obliged to pet him. "You like Joe, don't you?"

Hannah straightened. "Of course, I like him. He's a very likable man."

Lydia lifted one blonde brow. "And the fact he's as handsome as sin has nothing to do with your feelings."

"Nothing." Hannah sighed. "Joe is way out of my class. He's much too handsome for a fat, plain woman like me."

Lydia frowned. "I wish you'd stop referring to yourself like that. You're not fat. I know nearly every pound you carry is muscle. You're solidly built unlike me who is too thin. And you're definitely not plain."

Hannah let out a breath and shook her head. "But men like that you're slender. They want to feel protective of the little woman. You fit that bill and you're beautiful, besides. Perfect blonde hair, porcelain skin, no freckles—"

"Your freckles are cute and they make you anything but ordinary."

Hannah shrugged. "I know what I am. Men are not interested in me like that. Well, except Silas, my former employer. Most men want to be friends, maybe, like Gary did, but they don't want to court me or have me for a wife. As soon as they see you, it's bye bye Hannah. I should be jealous and once I was, but you can't help it you're beautiful or that Daddy loved you more."

"Now you're being ridiculous. Daddy loved you just as much as me, especially when you fixed his suits that the tailor couldn't. Besides, there will be plenty of men in Oregon Country who will want to marry you."

She sat up straight. "I won't marry, just to be married. I want to love my husband, not merely tolerate him."

Lydia cocked an eyebrow. "As I will, you mean."

"Lydie, I didn't—"

"I know you think I'm crazy, but I'm willing to take the chance Mr. Mosley and I will come to love each other. I simply have a different perspective about marriage than you do, and that's okay. We don't need to think the same way all the time."

Hannah nodded. "You're right. Now, I better go check on the animals and see if I can locate Mr.

Gunn to find out what we are supposed to do. Camp or travel."

She climbed down from the wagon box and went around the back of the wagon to where she tied the animals to a tree. She discovered one of the beef cows missing. The rope she'd tied it with lay on the ground.

"Damn." She pulled the animals behind the wagon and tied them to the rear rings put there for that specific purpose.

She was still cussing, albeit under her breath, when she came around the wagon.

"What's the matter that has you swearing?" asked Lydia.

"Oh, God, Lydie, we've lost one of the beef cattle. Stolen during the rainstorm. We'll have to spend some more of the money Mr. Mosley sent. Thank God for Mr. Walter Mosley."

"Who would steal one of our cows?"

"The Indians. Remember Mr. Gunn said they would pretty much ignore us, but might steal a cow or two. Well, they stole one of ours."

"What are we supposed to do about it?"

"I don't know if there's anything we can do. But we'll have to replace it as soon as we can. I'll talk to Mr. Gunn about buying a replacement when I ask him about camping for tonight. Maybe we'll run across a farmer or rancher that would be willing to sell us a cow."

Lydia nodded. "You better go talk to Mr. Gunn now."

"I'm on my way. If this is just the beginning of the journey what calamities can we expect for the rest of the distance?"

CHAPTER 4

Hannah walked toward the chuck wagon at the front of the train hoping she'd find Mr. Gunn there. She limped a little. Every footstep was painful, sending shooting pain up her foot to her ankle.

Now that the rain had stopped, everyone was out of their wagons, checking animals and making sure the wagons were not sunk in the mud. Sounds of people moving, shouting, children laughing, all quite normal on any given day, but because of the silence when the rain was falling, the daily sounds seemed loud.

She walked around people and animals as she slowly made her way to the chuck wagon.

Instead of Mr. Gunn, she found Joe and the cook, known as Cookie.

"We meet again, sir." Hannah raised her chin a smidge.

Joe was standing next to Cookie and they were drinking coffee. "So we do, Miss Granger."

She noticed he never used her given name around other people, always Miss Granger.

"Have you seen Mr. Gunn, *Mr. Stanton*?"

"Cookie and I were just discussing that very man. I'm still looking for him myself. As soon as I find him, I'll ask about camping here tonight. I'll let you know what he says…if that meets with your approval. Have you met Cookie? He's the camp cook."

"I have not." She extended her hand. "Pleased to meet you Mr. Cookie."

"Mr. Cookie. Isn't that a hoot. No lovely lady, my name is just Cookie."

"Very well, Cookie, it is." She turned her gaze on Joe. "That would be most agreeable. Would you also care to join us for supper this evening? Lydia said she'd heat the beans from last night and make fresh cornbread."

"As wonderful as that sounds, I am unfortunately previously engaged."

"Perhaps tomorrow then."

Joe frowned at her. "You should watch your provisions, you don't want to use them up too soon."

"I wouldn't ask you if we couldn't afford to feed you."

"In that case, I would be most honored."

"We'll see you at six."

"I'll be there."

"The reason I came to see Mr. Gunn is, we're missing a cow. I'm guessing the Indians took it during the rain storm. Do you know how we can replace it?"

"I don't but I'll ask Chester when I see him and let you know."

"Thank you." She turned to the cook. "It was very nice to meet you, Cookie."

The cook tipped his hat. "You, too, Miss."

Hannah turned and walked back to the wagon, head held high and trying not to limp...too much.

Cookie looked up at Joe.

"What in tarnation was that all about? Mr. Stanton and Miss Granger? I ain't blind I see you with those two females. I ain't never heard you talk like that before."

Joe grinned. "She's a little spitfire and was trying to show me she doesn't like me. But she does. She certainly does."

Cookie scratched his head.

"You younguns' are nuttier than a squirrel with his winter stash."

Joe watched Hannah leave, a smile on his face, wondering what she'd say if she knew he was having dinner with the Sandel women. They were lookers and he admitted he enjoyed looking, but not like with her.

What was he to do with Hannah?

Joe came by the wagon about an hour after Hannah returned.

"Chester says go ahead and make camp. He wants to let the road dry out some before we continue."

"Good. I wasn't looking forward to walking in this muck. What about the cow?"

"That he said we can't do anything about but try to get you a replacement if we come across a rancher willing to sell. I know of a couple of ranches we'll pass by, they might be able to accommodate you."

He stepped a little closer and lowered his voice.

"How are your feet?"

Hannah's heart pounded due to his close proximity. She smelled the rain and the man. She thought the scents were a very nice combination. "Not good, but not as bad as that first night."

"You should take the opportunity to clean them in the river again. I'll help you, if you like."

Remembering how much he'd helped her before, Hannah felt the burn in her cheeks.

"I...I shouldn't accept, but I will. I would be

pleased to have your assistance. Say seven-thirty, by the river."

"I'll be there. Bring more bandages so I can wrap your feet, plus the salve and soap to clean them."

"I will. Thank you, Joe. Or should I call you, Mr. Stanton?"

He chuckled. "Joe. Cookie thought we were crazy with our polite conversation earlier."

She laughed, enjoying the teasing conversation she had with Joe. No man had ever treated her like Joe. "I don't blame him. I felt pretty silly myself."

"Then why did you act all hoity-toity when you walked up?"

To hide her shaking hands she shoved them in the pockets of her skirt. "I...I don't know what you're talking about."

"Ah, there you go fibbin' again. And your blush has turned those pretty cheeks of yours a lovely pink."

Hannah looked at her feet, wishing the ground would open and just swallow her.

"Will you stop, please? All right I was a bit stiff. I didn't want Cookie to think poorly of me for being so familiar with you. I know I'm trying to leave the past behind, but it's difficult to just stop something that's been drummed into your head for too many years to count."

"And what do you want?"

"I want us to be friends. I want to be able to call you Joe any time I want."

"Then do it." He leaned a little closer. "I want to be much more than friends with you. Just so you know."

"What? With me? But...but...I'm so plain. You need someone beautiful—"

He stopped her speech with a tap on her nose.

"Are you fishing for compliments?"

"No."

"All right then, I think you're very attractive. I love your freckles and button nose. And your wild red hair—"

Indignant at his mention of her *red* hair, she corrected him. "It's strawberry blonde I'll have you know."

He laughed. "And you're funny and smart. You'll keep a man on his toes keeping up with your quick mind." He again tapped her on the nose. "See you at seven-thirty."

Hannah's mouth hung open as she watched him walk away and wondered what in the heck had just happened. Joe found her attractive? He was either lying, like most men, or needed spectacles.

Seven-twenty-five came and Hannah headed down to the river. She'd left Lydia getting ready for bed and gathered all of her supplies in a burlap bag then grabbed a lantern to light her way. As soon as she was out of sight of the wagon, she gave in to her pain and limped trying to find some relief.

When she reached the river, she looked around for Joe but didn't see him anywhere. *He probably changed his mind. I hope not, it's scary out here alone in the dark, even with the lantern.*

Undaunted, she still had to take the opportunity to cleanse her feet. She'd only done it twice since that first night and both times like now, she didn't have a choice. Her bandages were falling down around her boot tops and her socks weren't keeping them snug in her boots anymore either.

She sat on the grassy bank, the lantern next to her and removed her boots.

"Sorry, I'm late."

Hannah jumped nearly out of her skin, but she didn't shriek this time. She turned toward Joe who'd walked up behind her. "Do you have to do that?"

He lifted his hands and shrugged. "Do what?"

"Sneak up on me."

"I'm sorry. I didn't mean to startle you. As a bounty hunter, I'm trained not to make noise when I approach someone." He walked closer and knelt in front of her and finished removing her boot. "Shoot, Hannah, what have you been doing? How are you walking on these feet?"

"They're pretty much numb, and I didn't know the blisters were still this bad."

"Haven't you changed the bandages? You need to do that every day, if possible, but at least once a week. The country we're traveling through is easy compared to what is up ahead. We have ample water for you to take care of your feet while we follow the river. The desert ahead of us will not be so kind and you better have your feet healed by then. Now, let me unwrap these bandages."

She grimaced as he began working on her feet. "I've done them as often as I could."

He took off her socks and unwound the cloth quickly. When he got to her bare foot he sucked in a deep breath.

"You poor thing. Let's get you in the water. Did you bring your soap?"

She was on the verge of tears, not only was he lecturing her, but the feeling in her feet was returning and they hurt like hell. "I brought my soap and the salve. It's all there with the bandages."

The combination of the lantern and the moon gave them ample light to see and when Joe looked up he frowned.

"I'm sorry. I know you're doing the best you can. I'm just worried about you."

"That's nice of you and you're right. I should have been doing more. I just wanted to push through and didn't want Lydia to know. I don't want her walking and ending up with the same problem."

"Do her boots fit? If so, she won't have this problem." He pointed at her feet. "Yours are too big. You should try wearing two pairs of socks in addition to the bandages. Make the shoes tight so they don't rub. Let's go."

Joe bent down and scooped her into his arms. He moved as though she weighed no more than a child. She admitted she'd lost some weight, both she and Lydie had, but he'd done the same thing that first night. He was so strong. He made her feel positively petite.

He walked into the shallow water next to the bank, not too far out lest they get swept away by the current.

He set her on her feet. The bottom of the river was covered with rocks rather than mud. The stones made it harder to stand, because they were slick, but her feet would remain cleaner.

"I'll hold you while you wash your feet. Don't want you falling in the water now do we?"

"Thanks. Standing one-legged on the rocks while I wash my foot would be a lot harder, probably impossible, without your help."

She washed her feet as gently as she could and still get off the blood. When they were clean she washed out her socks.

"Good thing Lydia doesn't pay much attention to my wardrobe. She might realize that my socks are definitely the worse for wear."

When she'd finished washing her socks, he picked her up and carried her to the grassy bank.

"All right, lean back on your elbows and rest

your foot on my thigh. I'll do my best to be a gentleman."

She grinned. "I think you are a scoundrel. The nicest one I've ever met, but a scoundrel nonetheless."

He chuckled. "You know me so well."

While she got settled he picked up the bandage. He raised her skirt to her knee, wrapped her feet and put on her socks and boots.

"There, all better. I want you to stay off your feet as much as possible, please. They need a chance to heal."

She stood. "I can't and you know it."

He sighed, took off his hat and ran a hand through his hair. "I'll think of something. Trust me."

She cocked her head to the side. "But I do trust you, or you wouldn't be here now."

"I'll walk you back to your wagon."

She picked up the lantern. "Thanks. I'd appreciate that. It's a little scary out here at night."

"Why? We aren't even in Indian territory yet."

Hannah stopped walking. "Do you think we'll run into Indians? They did steal one of my cows, after all. Even if we aren't in Indian territory, they are still around here."

Joe shook his head. "Yes, they are but we won't see them. If they didn't take a cow sometimes, as you well know since they took one of yours, we'd never know they were around. But they won't attack a wagon train this big as long as everyone keeps up. Stragglers are vulnerable."

She started moving toward the wagons. "Then I'll have to make sure we are never a straggler."

"You're in the middle of the train. You should be safe unless…"

"Unless?"

He shrugged. "You lose a wheel or something else catastrophic."

She placed her right hand on his arm. "Good gracious, don't wish that upon us."

He shook his head. "I don't. Not on anyone."

They arrived back at the wagon and Hannah turned to Joe.

"Thank you, for all your help. I know I don't do it as well on my own."

"Anytime. Just let me know when."

"Thanks. I will." She turned and went around the wagon to the campfire which was burning down.

Lydia poked her head out from under the wagon.

"Oh, you're back. Are you coming to bed?"

"Not right away. You go ahead and go to sleep."

Hannah had too many things on her mind. Actually, she had only one thing on her mind…a man named Joe Stanton. There were only a few things that Hannah dreamed of, her own shop and a family with a handsome man like Joe, who loved her completely. Was that so much to ask?

She'd always dreamed of someone like Joe. Sinfully handsome, but kind and gentle. Now the real man was here and he said he liked her. But why? Why was he so nice to her? Was he really interested? Not possible. She wasn't beautiful like Lydia. She was just plain old Hannah.

Every man she'd known, and was possibly interested in, only wanted her as a friend. She had lots of male friends. They always wanted advice on how to get Lydia interested. She usually gave them the same old song and dance...candy, flowers, the theater...even though she knew those wouldn't make a difference.

Lydia was waiting for the thunderbolt to fall in love. That's why she'd agreed to marry Mr. Mosley, she didn't feel the pull of love and wasn't about to live in Independence with a young man she didn't love. Mr. Mosley, on the other hand, was old and she would care for him until his dying day. Then perhaps she'd just be the old lady with all the injured animals who lived down the lane. The crazy old lady they'd call her, and Hannah would be by her side, just as crazy as she was.

The thought filled her with melancholy. She knew she was falling in love with Joe. He was so different than any other man she'd known. He was kind and gentle, funny...he liked to tease her...and handsome as all get out. She was afraid to believe he could feel the same for her, even though he said he liked her. Could like turn to love?

The next morning Joe showed up before breakfast leading a beautiful, caramel colored horse with a white mane.

Hannah greeted him. "Well, hello this fine morning. Did you come to join us for breakfast? We haven't started the Johnny cakes yet. We have plenty of batter and some blueberry syrup Lydia made from the berries she picked at our last camp."

Joe took the horse over and tied him to their wagon.

Hannah followed him. "Where is that big black horse you usually ride? Did you get a new horse? It's beautiful." She walked up to the animal and stroked its neck.

"In a manner of speaking, I did get a new horse. I'm borrowing her from the horses Chester brought along to switch out with, so no one animal gets too tired. And I'd love to join you for breakfast, if you're sure you don't mind."

"Oh, please. You have an open invitation. Anytime you want a meal with us, just stop by. It's the least I can do to repay you for your kindness."

Hanna got a tin cup and poured Joe a cup of fresh coffee. They would keep the same pot, drinking from it at noon and supper, until it was gone. They didn't waste the precious beverage.

Coffee was too hard to come by out here. They'd been traveling for three weeks now and were about two-hundred and fifty miles northwest of Independence. They'd followed the Little Blue River until it connected with the Platte River. Now they followed the Platte ever westward toward Oregon Country.

The country they passed through was beautiful. Mostly untamed. It was green because it was spring, mostly flat with a few places of rolling hills. The grass was tall and provided lots of food for the oxen, cows, and horses, saving on the amount of hay they needed.

Trees lined the rivers. Some she could identify: oak, willow, cottonwood, and a maple or two. Others she'd never seen. Tall ones with white bark and leaves that quaked in the wind.

She handed Joe the cup and then sat on a bucket across the fire from him, picked up her cup and took a sip. "So why did you bring the horse here?"

"She's for you."

Her eyes widened. "For me? But I don't know how to ride a horse. I've never been on one in my life."

"About time you learned." He leaned forward and whispered so only she could hear. "I want you off your feet, remember?"

"Of course, I remember," she hissed, looking over her shoulder to see where Lydia was. She was relieved to see she was next to the wagon and wouldn't overhear. "But don't you think it looks a little suspicious with you spending all this time with me? People are liable to think you are interested in me."

He smiled. "And they wouldn't be wrong."

Hannah dropped her coffee cup and narrowed. "Are you sure? I thought you were just being nice before. Is that what you're doing now?"

"Nope. I like you, Hannah Granger. I hope you like me, too."

Hannah nodded. Her spilled coffee forgotten. "I do. I just thought you would be more interested in Lydia, she's so—"

"If you say beautiful and that you're plain, I'm leaving. You are not plain. I thought I made that clear."

"Well, you did, but I believed you were just being nice so you could get to know Lydia. That's what most men do."

He set his cup on the ground and stood over her. "I'm never *nice* when it comes to you. And I'm not interested in Lydia and I'm not most men. Let's get you on that horse and see if you can stay on."

Hannah took a deep breath, nodded and stood. "All right, if you say so."

They walked over to the horse. Joe untied it, crossing the reins over the animal's neck, just in front of the saddle.

"Oh, what a beautiful animal."

Hannah turned at the feminine voice.

Behind her stood the women from the Bond wagon. Both of them beautiful with pale skin and shiny brown hair that was getting blonde streaks in it from the sun. They almost looked like twins but were actually unrelated. Malena Farrow had the darker hair and brown eyes and she was about two inches taller than Carole. Both wore simple calico dresses, Carole in blue and Malena in pink.

"Hello, Malena. Carole. How are you?"

"We're fine," responded Carole, the older of the two women and the shorter one as well. "We just had to come admire the horse. He's a beauty."

"She's a mare," said Joe. "Her name is Maisy."

"Of course," said Malena, who tittered behind her hand.

The women stayed for a few minutes admiring Maisy and, in Hannah's opinion, Joe, too.

"Excuse us, ladies," said Joe. "I've some teaching to do. You can visit Maisy at another time."

"Oh, of course. Forgive us. We just had to come and see her."

They turned and headed back across the corral to their wagon.

"Now, where were we? Oh, yes. Maisy's a good horse. This is how you mount. Put your left foot in the stirrup, grab the saddle horn and the back of the saddle to pull yourself up. Lift your right leg and swing it over the horses back where you then place your right foot in that stirrup." He picked up the reins and sat on the horse for a moment before dismounting. "Now let's see you try."

Hannah took a deep breath and lifted her leg until her foot reached the stirrup. She grabbed the saddle where he'd indicated and pulled herself up and over landing on her belly. Next, she stood in the stirrup and lifted her right leg over the saddle. Finally, she was seated and she grinned down at Joe. "I did it." Suddenly she started to slip to her right. She gasped and grabbed for the pommel.

Joe pulled her upright. "Did you put your foot in the stirrup?"

"I forgot. I was too amazed I'd managed to sit without falling off. Guess I almost did, didn't I?"

"You did. Now I want you to dismount and try it again. This time, don't forget the right stirrup."

"All right. I won't."

She climbed down and remounted again and again until Joe was satisfied she could do it on her own.

"I'll teach you how to saddle her tomorrow morning. Tonight, I'll come by and take care of her. You can watch to see what I do so you know how."

"Since you're coming by anyway, why don't you come for supper?"

"I'd like to, but I'm otherwise engaged."

The spear of jealousy lanced through her, unbidden and unwanted. "Oh. Well, that's fine. You must be in high demand as a dinner companion." She tried hard to sound aloof but couldn't manage it.

Joe grinned. "Jealous are we?"

Hannah raised her chin. "Of course, not. Why would I be? It's not like we're courting after all."

He stopped smiling. "No, we're not."

"There, you see. All is well." She could kick herself. He knew she liked him now. If she was honest with herself, she more than liked him. Was she the wounded animal and Joe was Lydia, taking in the animal and healing it?

CHAPTER 5

True to his word Joe came by that night and showed her how to care for the horse. She would have to take away hay from the cows, but the prairie grasses were abundant and would feed the both the milk cow and the remaining beef cow, the oxen and the horse for the most part.

He stayed around for coffee and biscuits with honey for dessert.

Hannah didn't understand him. He said he was interested in her, but not in courting. After all, she'd given him ample opportunity to ask to court her. He confused her. On top of the she wasn't sure what she wanted from him. To be more than his friend that was for sure. But she knew he didn't even consider marriage at all given his profession? Hadn't he told Chester he wasn't the marrying kind?

"So let me understand this," Lydia with one arm crossed over her waist and the hand with fingers at her chin. "Hannah will ride the horse now instead of walk?"

"That's correct," said Joe.

Lydia furrowed her brows. "Couldn't she just ride in the wagon with me? At least when we aren't both walking with the oxen. I just learned not to use the lines but to crack the whip over the animals' heads to make them go the way I want. It's actually much easier on me, and probably on them."

Joe shook his head. "Hannah needs to learn how to handle a horse. You might have need of one when you get to Oregon City or even before when we cross the mountains. Better to learn to ride now on the open, flat prairie, than later in the mountains."

Hannah listened to the exchange between her sister and Joe. Lydia was asking all the questions, Hannah expected her to. Everything Hannah herself wanted to know but was too embarrassed to ask.

Hannah swallowed her biscuit. "So you'll come by in the morning before breakfast and show me how to put the equipment on the horse, right? Will you stay for breakfast?"

"That's right and I was hoping you'd ask me to eat with you. But I don't want to use up your supplies. I'll bring the bacon."

"That would be most appreciated."

She beamed; happy he wanted to spend more time with them even if it was just because Lydia was the best cook on the train...in Hannah's opinion.

Joe left to do his turn at guard duty. Mr. Gunn posted guards every night, just to watch for anything that might affect the train, whether it was hostile Indians, weather, prairie fires, or outlaws looking to make an easy score. His outriders all seemed to be good honest men that he'd worked with before. If Joe was an example they were all crack shots. At least she thought he must be, given his occupation.

Hannah helped Lydia make their bed. The night was beautiful and they opted to sleep under the stars.

She laid there looking at the magnificent sky, filled with sparkling specks of light against the inky black. She recognized a couple of constellations. The Big Dipper, Little Dipper, and Orion were easy to spot. Their old neighbor in Independence, a retired astronomy teacher, had owned a telescope. He would aim it at an area of the sky and then have her look, telling her what she was seeing. He taught her a lot and was a very kind man, reminding her of her father.

She wondered if Joe would be a good father. Why she was thinking about that now, she had no idea. Then she admitted she lied to herself. The more she got to know Joe, the more she fell in love with him. These feelings were so much more intense than when she thought she'd fallen in love with Gary. That had been nothing. Oh, she was hurt to be used again to get to Lydia. This time it would hurt like crazy when Joe told her he didn't feel the same way.

Before breakfast, Joe arrived to show her how to saddle Maisy. First, he put on the bridle, careful to place the bit behind the horse's teeth and leather straps over her ears. Then he laid the blanket on the horse's back to protect her from saddle sores. After he was sure the blanket was flat he threw one the saddle and tightened the cinches, making sure the mare didn't bloat which would make the saddle loose when she quit holding her breath.

He patted the horse on the rump. "I'll come back when everyone is ready to pull out and make sure you can get on Maisy by yourself."

Hannah ran her hand along Maisy's neck. The hair was short but soft and the horse liked it enough that she nudged her with her nose when Hannah stopped.

"Maisy's a good horse. Treat her right and she'll treat you right."

"Thanks for everything. I don't know how to repay you?"

"Go for a walk with me after supper tonight?"

She clasped her hands behind her to stop them from shaking. "I'd like that very much."

Hannah dressed with care for supper that night. She put on her second best dress, a blue calico, and took her shawl to keep warm.

After dinner, Joe stood. "Are you ready for our walk, Hannah?"

"Yes."

Lydia cocked her head and narrowed her eyes, smiled and then stood. "Do I need to come along as a chaperone with you kids?"

Hannah shook her head. "We are long past being kids."

Joe chuckled. "I promise to take good care of her and bring her back at a reasonable hour."

"Oh, go on. Enjoy yourselves." Lydia took all their supper dishes over to the wagon to wash them. "I'm not Hannah's mother. She can take care of herself and I know you are a gentleman."

Hannah and Joe walked out of the wagon circle and Joe led them toward the river. The moon gave them plenty of light to walk by, so they hadn't taken a lantern.

When they got to the river's edge, the moon glinted off the rushing water making the liquid look like it was dancing.

Joe took Hannah's hand. "With you, I don't

want to be a gentleman. I want to kiss you in a most *ungentlemanly* way."

Hannah cast her gaze toward the ground. She'd never been kissed before. What if she was bad at it? If she didn't try it, how would she know? She looked up at him. "Then what are you waiting for?"

He smiled and pulled her close. When her body was flush with his, he dipped his head and pressed his lips upon hers. He sipped at her and when he pressed his tongue against the seam of her lips, she opened them in surprise. Joe entered her mouth, tasting her, circling her tongue with his, and challenging her.

Hannah responded, tentatively at first. Her tongue touched his and then pulled back.

He held her closer and tighter, so she felt his hard body all along her softer one.

She wrapped her arms around his neck and fully responded to his kiss. She welcomed the feel of his lips, firm and yet, soft, too. She wound her fingers in his hair which touched his shoulders now. Silky and not what she expected.

Joe pulled back and grinned. "I knew you'd be passionate. You please me very much, Hannah Granger. Very much, indeed."

She kept her arms around his neck, enjoying him holding her close. With his strong arms around her waist she felt safe. "Why did you kiss me? I mean, I'm very glad you did, but why? Why me?

There are so many more beautiful women on this train. Carole Bond and Malena Farrow for instance. I saw the way they looked at you this morning... like they wanted to have you as the main entrée at supper."

Joe laughed. "You have a way with words." He sobered, and his eyes bore into her depths. "Hannah, you are beautiful. Not only on the outside but on the inside, where it is much more important. You go in pain, rather than cause your sister any worry. You let your feet bleed, rather than let your sister walk. As far as I'm concerned, you are an amazing woman. And I notice that even though you may want to give Lydia a hard time about caring for wounded animals, you love them as much as she does. And most important," he smiled. "You are an honorable woman."

Hannah was humbled. Never had a man complimented her with such fervor. "I don't do anything more or less than anyone else."

"Oh, yes, you do. Most of the women on this wagon train are out for themselves and no one else. Believe me. I know. I've been propositioned by at least half of these women, even though they are promised to another. Not keeping their word is not honorable. When you and Lydia give your word, you keep it. I like that."

"Thank you. That is how we were raised. Papa used to tell us all the time, "Your word is your bond. When you give it, you better mean it." We've always only given our word when we could keep it. Lydia has given her word to marry Mr. Walter Mosley when we reach Oregon City and she will, no matter what. I know that and so does she."

"But what about you? What about Hannah Granger? What will she do in Oregon City?"

Joe continued to hold her in his arms and she wasn't about to pull away. She felt more at home, or peace or just plain comfortable there than anywhere else. "I want to open a dress shop. These women will want new clothes and I make the best."

"You could do that. I think you will be good at whatever you do."

Her eyes widened. "You do?"

"Yes."

"Why?"

He cocked his eyebrow. "Because you are determined."

"I am."

He grinned. "And stubborn."

She frowned. "I'm not."

"Be honest."

She released a short breath and rolled her eyes. "Oh, all right. I can be stubborn about certain things. But only when I'm in the right."

Joe laughed but didn't let her go. "When have you ever thought you were not right about something?"

She tilted her head and then looked up at the stars and smiled. "Well, never."

"See? That's what I thought."

Hannah gazed up into his face, illuminated by the moon, he definitely looked sinful and her heartbeat raced. "Joe. Would you kiss me again?"

He let out a breath. "I thought you'd never ask."

When their lips merged this time, she touched him with her tongue first. She felt him smile before answering with his own.

When they finally broke apart, both breathless.

"You'll be the death of me," whispered Joe.

"I was thinking the same about you. We are quite the pair."

"How are your feet?"

"I'm surviving. I think riding Maisy will make a big difference. Thank you."

"You're welcome. I should take you back."

"Yes, I suppose we should. Lydia may say she won't worry, but she will."

As they walked back into the circle by the Granger wagon, they saw Lydia bending over something.

When they got closer, Hannah saw Lydia petting a small dog.

At their approach, she stood, turned and smiled. "Look what I found. This little guy has been following us for days, but I've always had to put his food outside the corral. This time he came inside to me."

Joe narrowed his eyes and stared at the pup. "Lydia, that's a wolf. Don't you know that they're dangerous?"

She shrugged. "He's not a danger to anyone. He's alone and much too young to survive out here by himself."

Joe took a deep breath and shook his head. Then he glanced at Hannah.

"Is she always collecting stray animals?"

Hannah nodded. "Always. Since she was a child she brought home abandoned or wounded animals. She heals them, and they usually decide to stay. We had to find homes for a dozen cats, dogs, and other critters before we left. Maybe more."

His eyes were narrowed as he watched Lydia and the pup. "Well, I hope she knows what she's doing."

Hannah stood next to Joe and watched him, watch Lydia. She smiled. "She does. Believe me, they'll be okay and she'll teach the pup manners so he doesn't scare people as he grows."

Joe sighed. "All right, but the first time that pup goes after someone, he'll have to go."

"I understand." Hannah's smile widened. "But he won't. You'll see."

Joe raised her hand to his lips and kissed the top. "Thank you for a wonderful walk. Would you care to go again tomorrow?"

"I'd love that." *My feet may not like it, but I will. If I can walk next to a wagon all day, I can walk next to Joe for a short time at night.*

"Good."

He turned, gave another look at Lydia and the pup, and then walked away shaking his head.

Hannah went over to Lydia as she knelt next to the little gray pup with black above both eyes like brows and white socks on his hind legs.

He must have been the runt of the litter or he's a lot younger than I would have thought possible to be out here alone. "How long have you been feeding him?"

"About a week. I had to win him over."

"How old do you figure he is?"

"Two months maybe. Perhaps his mother was killed while they were out alone." Lydia pet the wolf while he licked clean the plate of food she gave him. "That's the only reason I can see why he would be alone. They travel in packs and the rest of the pack would normally care for him, but there have never been any other animals about when I feed him. Just him."

"Where will you have him sleep? Trinity probably won't like him."

Lydia shrugged and picked up the pup.

He started licking her face.

"He'll just have to learn to share me."

"True. I doubt very seriously if these are the last animals you'll collect on this trip. They seem to know where to find you."

She laughed. "I know. Isn't that funny how they do that?"

Hannah shook her head and rolled her eyes. "I'm going to bed."

"You go ahead. The pallets and blankets are out by the fire."

"We get to Fort Laramie soon, maybe tomorrow. We should inventory and see what we need."

Lydia let the squirming pup down.

He immediately ran to Hannah and barked.

She smiled and petted the little thing. He started wagging his tail and licked her hand.

Lydia ticked off items they needed with her fingers. "Well, we're out of eggs and bacon. Our flour and sugar both need to be replenished. We need cornmeal and coffee. Basically, we need everything and if they have any potatoes and carrots, I want some of those for stew. The only things we don't need yet are dried beans and lard. And I want to get more than we started with since we are mostly feeding Joe at meals now and we have the animals to feed. I'm so thankful, Walter sent enough money for us to have plenty of food on our journey."

Hannah nodded. "So am I. I suggest we get to the store early. Everyone else will want the same things and the fort might not have enough to supply us all."

"You can ride ahead on that horse, give them the order and pay for it. I'll bring the wagon in as soon as I can."

"I will, if I can manage to get the horse moving at more than a walk or a trot. I'd rather ride in the wagon than have her trot."

"Let's just hope the fort is well provisioned."

"What will we do if it isn't?"

"I don't know."

The next morning Hannah could hardly move. Her legs and back were sore and the thought of another day on the horse made her hurt even worse.

Joe came by, as was becoming his custom, before breakfast and saddled Maisy. This morning he tied leather bags to the back of the saddle.

She pointed. "What are those?"

"My saddle bags. I'm going on a buffalo hunt with some of the other men and I don't want to get blood all over them carrying back the meat."

She rubbed her back trying to relieve some of the pain. "Oh, all right."

Joe frowned as he gazed at her. "What's the matter?"

"My legs and back are sore from riding. I'm almost ready to call it quits."

He smiled. "Everyone gets sore from spending all day in the saddle for the first few days. Doesn't matter how well you ride or how used you are to riding. You have to keep riding though, or you'll be sore like this every time you ride. You don't want to always be in pain after you ride, do you?"

Hannah shook her head. "Heavens, no. I'll keep on so I get my body use to the abuse."

Joe wrapped his arm around her shoulders and squeezed her. "That's my girl."

Hannah's head snapped up. *His girl? Does he mean it or is it just a saying? Do I really want to know?*

CHAPTER 6

June 29, 1852

It was mid-afternoon and Hannah was bored and curious. The prairie here in the Nebraska Territory was not awe inspiring. The grasses were brown, the rivers they passed or crossed were shallow. The oxen hadn't even slowed when they hit the water. Very few trees here and those she did see were usually at the river's edge.

She glanced again at the saddlebags behind her. What did Joe keep in those? They weren't big enough for a change of clothes; at least, they didn't look like it to her.

She loosely tied the reins around the saddle horn and turned so she could open one of the bags. Knowing she was snooping and shouldn't do it only stopped her for a moment.

Inside Hannah found a stack of paper. She pulled out the top sheet and saw it was a poster with a drawing of a man, a line saying why he was wanted and by whom. Then below were the amount of the bounty...two-hundred-fifty dollars, and the words Dead or Alive. That was a lot of money for one man. Then she saw he was wanted for murder.

Those posters were of people wanted for various crimes. She quickly put back the paper and tied the bag closed. Suddenly ashamed of what she'd done she tried to forget the face she saw. Only she couldn't because she'd seen that face before. The man was on the wagon train, she was sure of it. She needed to tell Joe but she didn't want to admit what she'd done.

What in the heck would she do now?

Joe came by before supper and brought a roast of fresh meat with him. The men had killed a buffalo and having processed the animal, they were passing out the meat to each of the wagons.

Lydia took the offering from him and put it in a pot. "We'll have it tonight for supper. No more beans. I still have a few potatoes and biscuits, of course, with the last of the honey. I'll cut half into steaks and we'll have a grand dinner and tomorrow I'll roast it over the open fire. You're coming aren't you Joe?"

Joe nodded. "Wouldn't miss it, Lydia. We're coming into Fort Laramie tomorrow. We'd hoped to make it today, but the buffalo hunt was more important." He looked over at Hannah. "Would you care to take a walk after dinner, Hannah?"

Heat filled her cheeks and she nodded. "I'd like that very much."

"Good. We have some things to discuss."

Oh, God. He knows.

"All right."

Dinner was grand. Hannah realized she was hungrier than she thought and the meal was very satisfying. Meat was something they hadn't had for a while.

I can only eat beans for so long before I'd almost rather go hungry.

Joe rubbed circles on his stomach. "Lydia, I'd be glad to help with the dishes after such a fine meal."

She waved him off. "I can do these in no time. You and Hannah go for your walk."

Joe gazed at Hannah. "Are you ready?"

"Let me get my shawl."

He winked at her. "You won't need one."

Hannah felt heat rise up from her chest to her forehead. "I'm ready then."

He held out his arm.

She put a hand through the crook in his elbow.

Joe grabbed a lantern as he and Hannah stepped away from the wagon into the night. As had become their ritual, he called to Lydia, "I won't keep her out too late."

"I'm not worried," returned Lydia, as always.

Hannah held on to Joe's arm with both hands. "Where are we headed tonight?"

"To a little grove of trees not far from here. I thought they would give us the privacy we need."

"Privacy?" She swallowed hard.

"Yes, privacy. I don't want anyone else to know. Do you?"

Hannah looked around and her heart beat rapidly. She answered with as much eagerness as she could muster. "Of course, not."

When they reached the trees, Joe found a patch of long June grass.

"Let's sit, shall we?"

Hannah sat and arranged her skirts around her. "Don't we have to lay down for this?"

Joe leaned his back against a tree and stretched his long legs out in front of him. Then he gazed at her and laughed.

"We're not making love. Not tonight. When we make love, I want a bed not a patch of grass."

She looked down at her lap and clasped her hands to stop them from shaking. "Oh. Then you do want to make love to me?"

He reached over and with a finger to her chin,

lifted her head until she gazed at him. "Very much. Tonight, though, I want to talk about my saddle bags. You were into them. I could tell by the way the strings were tied in a bow."

Hannah hung her head and picked at her skirt. "I was curious to see what a man like you carries." She raised her head. "I'm sorry, I shouldn't have let my curiosity control me."

"You're right you shouldn't but you've been... wary...since I got back. Was it something you saw on the posters or just guilt?"

She let out a breath and looked up at him. "Both, but mostly I didn't know how to tell you...the man on the poster I saw is on this wagon train. I'd swear to it."

"Who? I know that Mr. Smith and Mr. Jones are not who they seem. Was the drawing of one of them or someone else?"

"Really? Oh my. That's makes three. I only saw the top poster and it was Mr. O'Toole, just four wagons behind ours. I don't think he suspects anything. He's been very polite."

"That poster was for Dick Lancaster, wanted for murdering his wife, Dead or Alive, if I remember correctly."

"That's right. Have you memorized all those posters?"

He shook his head and rolled a piece of the long, thin grass between his thumb and forefinger. "The newest ones are in the back and I haven't gotten to those yet." He put the grass in his mouth and chewed on the end.

"What are we to do about Mr. O'Toole?"

"Nothing."

"Nothing?" She widened her eyes and tilted her head. "We can't just do *nothing*. He murdered his wife, for Pete's sake."

He shrugged. "Perhaps. But I have nowhere to keep him until we reach Fort Laramie tomorrow. Then I'll talk to the post commander. He might not want the responsibility of taking him back to stand trial."

"How can you be so nonchalant?" She stopped and thought about what he said. "You mean he hasn't been convicted yet? Then why is Dead or Alive on the poster?"

He took the grass out of his mouth. "Because he ran rather than face a jury. Running usually means they're guilty."

She leaned on the grass with a hand and picked pieces with the other. "I suppose, but somehow Dead or Alive, feels wrong."

"The method of capture on the poster is not my concern. I just take them back. Alive, if possible, but I won't take a bullet if they try to kill me instead of returning."

"I should hope not. Does that happen often? Them trying to kill you?"

"More often than you might think. Each of them knows what awaits them if they go back. Either a rope or a jury. Would you want to give up your freedom? Would you simply comply and return or would you fight like hell to stay free?"

She sighed. "Freedom. I understand more about what you do now. Your line of work is indeed very dangerous."

"That's why I can't take a wife. I can't put any woman through that worry."

She felt a stab in her heart hearing his words and then looked up into his blue eyes. "I suppose not. But what if she would rather be with you sometimes than not at all?"

"I especially couldn't do it then. The woman would care for me and, more than likely, I for her. Leaving her alone for months at a time wouldn't be fair."

Hannah leaned forward, determined to make him see it was possible for him to marry...her. "But what if she were to ride with you?"

Joe laughed, but without humor. "The life I lead is too hard for most women. Sleeping on the ground, eating jerky and hardtack for days on end. Lucky to have a bath once a month and that probably in a river somewhere. You wouldn't have a wagon to take shelter in. You'd ride whether it was raining or snowing or dry out. You ride until your body can't stand it and then you walk. Can you really see yourself living like that, all the time, not just for a few months on a wagon train?"

Hannah lowered her gaze and was quiet. *Even*

being with Joe wouldn't compensate for living that hard life, he's right I would hate it.

"That's what I thought."

He smiled.

But Hannah thought it was a sad smile.

She raised her chin a little. "You're right, I probably wouldn't like living that way, but I'd do it to be with you."

He stared—really looked, and then his mouth turned down. "I believe you would, but what kind of a man would I be to subject you to living in that way? What about children? We couldn't be taking them bounty hunting."

Sadness filled her. "Couldn't you do something else? Be a sheriff somewhere or open a mercantile or something?"

"I intend to retire someday. When I have enough money saved, I want to start a cattle ranch in Utah Territory on the Rio Grande in the Sangre De Cristo Mountains or maybe raise horses somewhere else. I don't know yet."

He's thought this out for a long time and knows what his goal is. And it is nothing like mine. "How long will that be?"

"Another few bounties."

Her hopes grew. Could he retire soon? "Are you talking years or months?

He broke the blade. "I don't know."

Her heart broke at his words and she knew he was telling her the truth. He didn't know.

"With Lancaster, there are three wanted men on this wagon train and I can't handle three men alone. I'll have to leave Lancaster for another town or lose him when we get to Oregon City if they won't honor the bounties here."

"Maybe I—"

His eyes narrowed. "No!"

Hannah jumped. He'd practically yelled.

He sat up, spine straight. "I don't want you anywhere near any of these men. Be polite if you see them. Don't do anything different. If they get the idea that you are aware of their deception, they'll run and I don't want to chase them when I have them all right here."

She let out a breath and nodded. "I won't give myself away. I don't have much interaction with the bank robbers, at least so far. And Mr. O'Toole has been nice when we cross paths, but keeps mostly to himself."

"Good. Leave it that way."

He reached over, took her hand and squeezed it. "I don't want anything to happen to you."

Hannah smiled and looked down at their hands. "You know, people on the wagon train think we're courting."

Joe brought her hand to his lips and kissed the top. "Maybe we are. I don't deny that I'm very attracted to you, Hannah."

She shifted her gaze back to his. "I want marriage and all the good and bad times that go with it."

He pulled back his hand.

"You know I can't give you that."

A tear escaped her eye and rolled down her cheek, landing on top of his hand. "And I can't give you the gift I'm saving for my husband, as much as I might want to."

"I know and I respect you for your moral fiber and determination. As much as I want you, I couldn't take your treasure. I'm an honorable man."

"I know you are. Thank you, for respecting my beliefs. We should probably get back."

"You're right."

He stood and extended his hand to her.

She took it. His hand was warm, even out in the cool air.

He pulled her to her feet then picked up the lantern and gave her his arm.

She took it and against all that she'd been taught about decorum, she leaned into him. His scent surrounded her. He smelled clean, like he'd just bathed. She recognized sandalwood, her favorite scent for a man. He must have shaved before he came to dinner and used cologne after.

"I probably shouldn't be taking you for walks anymore."

"Probably not, but I hope you do. I enjoy talking to you."

"And I, you. But aren't you worried people will still believe I'm courting you?"

81

"They will think what they want to regardless of what we do. I know because they gossiped about my father being so close to my aunt, my mother's sister. They said things like he had two wives and so forth, just because he was nice to her and helped her when my uncle died. Besides, I know there are a couple of women who, brides or not, would be happy to take you into their bed. I'm a jealous woman, as you've seen, whether we are just friends or more. I'd rather you spent your time with me."

He chuckled. "You would, would you?"

"I do." *I want to say those words while standing next to you in front of a preacher. There was one on the train. Reverend Trowbridge. He and his family were headed to Oregon City to set up a church.*

"What are you thinking about?"

"Nothing important."

They were just about to the wagons but still covered by darkness.

He stopped and faced her. "I want to kiss you."

She reached up and cupped his jaw. "I want you to kiss me."

He blew out the lantern and lowered his head to hers. He took her lips with his; gentle at first, then he rubbed his tongue across the seam of her closed lips.

She gasped, the sensation always a surprise.

He pressed forward and tangled with her tongue. They danced and fought and tasted.

He broke the kiss.

She leaned back in his arms. "You give me the most amazing kisses. Each one has been wonderful and yet different from the others. That one was an incredible kiss, especially for my third."

"You've never been kissed before me?"

"I never wanted to kiss anyone before."

"Too bad that was our last kiss. I can't take the chance I'll ruin your reputation."

Hannah peered around his shoulder. "We might be too late for that situation. Look." She pointed to where Reverend Trowbridge stood with his arms crossed over his chest.

Joe cursed and turned around. "Evening, reverend. Beautiful night."

"It was. What do you propose to do about what I and any number of other people on this train, saw?"

Joe shoved Hannah behind him.

She stood close and peeked around his arm, embarrassed, but excited as well.

"What do you think you saw?"

The reverend stood nearly as tall as Joe but was very thin. His brown hair, streaked liberally with gray was cut so he sported mutton chop sideburns. "I saw you and Miss Granger wrapped in each other's arms, *kissing*."

Hannah felt Joe's back straighten.

The reverend stood taller, his back stiff like a broomstick was down it. "You know that decent folk don't do that unless they're courting and even then a chaperone should accompany you."

Joe took a deep breath and crossed his arms over his chest. "What do you propose?"

"You marry right away. Once you're married, no one will think twice about your actions."

Hannah couldn't believe her ears. Marry Joe. Her dreams, her hopes were all coming true, but so were her fears. She didn't want to marry Joe out of necessity because of her reputation. She wanted him to want her, for her, to love her. She couldn't in good consciousness marry him.

Joe tensed and stood there for a minute. Then he turned to Hannah. He took her hand. "Will you marry me?"

Hannah looked into the face of the man she loved. With just one little word, all her dreams would come true. She reached up, her heart breaking, smiled and cupped his jaw. "No."

Joe rolled his eyes. "Hannah, you can't say 'no'. Your reputation will be ruined."

"I doubt that. The only person who saw us kiss was Reverend Trowbridge." She turned her gaze toward the reverend. "And he won't say anything. Will you, Reverend?"

"I...I...uh—" The reverend pulled on his collar to loosen it.

"How can you be sure no one else saw us?" asked Joe, looking over his shoulder.

"Well, I—" *What if someone else did? Would being*

caught kissing Joe really ruin my reputation? She knew the answer before she asked herself the question. Yes, it would, and that could hinder her future ambitions'

"If I'd known she was so easy to kiss and get away with it, I'd have gotten a couple of kisses myself. Maybe something more." Suddenly, from out of the darkness behind them, stepped Dick Bailey, the outrider she'd met the first day of the journey. The lanky man sauntered forward and stood just a few steps from the other three.

Joe moved Hannah out of Bailey's view.

"That's my fiancée you are talking about, Bailey. I suggest you apologize."

"Don't sound to me like she's gonna marry you, Joe. That makes her fair game for the rest of us."

Joe launched himself at Bailey and knocked him to the ground. Then he stood with his fists raised. "Come on, Bailey. Don't have what it takes to back up your foul words?"

Bailey swung at Joe.

Joe blocked Bailey's punch with his left forearm and threw a second right to the man's jaw.

Bailey turned his head and moved his jaw back and forth as though testing to see if anything was broken. Hannah was surprised that he didn't appear to be injured.

Then he smiled and hit Joe with a left hook to his jaw, followed by a right jab to his stomach.

From the blows Joe backed up two steps.

Bailey reached for his gun.

Joe drew faster and shot the gun from Bailey's hand.

The man grabbed his wounded hand with the other, looked at it and then raised his gaze to Joe. "Now, look what you done."

"Leave and don't come back. If I see your face again, I'll kill you."

"All right. I'm goin'. I'm goin'."

Bailey turned, found his gun, picked it up with his left hand and hurried away.

Hannah ran to Joe. "Are you all right? You're bleeding." She lifted a hand to his face.

Joe grabbed her hand.

"I'm fine and we're getting married tomorrow. I won't hear another contrary word about it."

Hannah lowered her hand, clasped it with the other and looked down, but nodded.

Joe lifted her chin with a knuckle.

"Getting married is for the best for both of us. If you don't marry me, then I'm the callous man who took advantage of your good nature and you're the loose woman who let me. Don't you see? Both of us are stuck with this marriage, whether we want it or not."

Reverend Trowbridge, who hadn't moved and whose eyes were wide, cleared his throat and regained his composure.

"I'll see you two tomorrow morning at my wagon. Six o'clock sharp."

"Yes, sir," said Hannah."

"We'll be there," said Joe.

"Now," said the reverend. "I'll return to my wagon. The train is usually moving by seven and we want the celebration to be over with in plenty of time to get ready to move out. Six o'clock sharp. Be there."

"Yes, sir," said Hannah.

"We'll be there," said Joe.

The reverend put his hands in his pockets. "I'll return to my wagon. I'm afraid my evening stroll no longer appeals."

"Goodnight, reverend," said Joe.

"Goodnight, sir," said Hannah.

Joe reached for her hand. "Let's get you to your wagon and let your sister know she's attending a wedding tomorrow."

Hannah gazed up at Joe, tears filled her eyes but she refused to let them fall. "I'm sorry. This entire situation is my fault."

One side of his mouth turned down and he sighed. "No, it's not. It's mine. I know better than to let myself be lured by a pretty face."

"Don't worry." Hannah gazed out at the darkness, her heart breaking. *I love Joe. I never wanted to marry him this way and I won't make him stay in a marriage he doesn't want.* "We can get the marriage annulled when we reach Oregon City."

"Regardless of what you think, I don't take this lightly. I was raised that marriage is forever. We're stuck together, Hannah, whether you like it or not. We'll tell Lydia together. Come on." He placed a hand at the small of her back and finished walking to the wagon.

Hannah wiped away her tears and fell into step next to Joe. She glanced up at the man she would call husband.

Now that we're getting married, I'll ride with him bounty hunting. I can watch his back and cook for him. We'll keep each other company. I know how to shoot, maybe not as well as Joe, but I could shoot rabbits and stuff for food. I know we can do it if he'll let me.

Can we have a real marriage or is that just a dream?

CHAPTER 7

July 3, 1852

Joe rode on his big black horse and arrived at five-thirty for breakfast as had become his habit. Today though, besides being earlier than usual, he wore a white shirt, black wool pants, and vest. He was clean-shaven except his mustache, even the little bit of stubble he had last night was gone.

Hannah thought he looked wonderful, though she liked the way he looked before he shaved even more.

She and Lydia wore their best dresses. Because Hannah had worked as a seamstress in a tailor shop, she sewed all their dresses and they bought more luxurious material with the money they saved. Hannah's dress was pale pink silk which, according to Lydia, made her skin glow. She had to admit being rosy-cheeked with her green eyes sparkling, she thought she looked prettier than she ever had before.

Lydia's dress was silk, too. Pale blue, it was to be her wedding dress but she wore it today in celebration of Hannah and Joe's nuptials.

Joe approached Lydia and placed light kisses on both her cheeks. Then he grinned. "Hello, my soon-to-be sister. You look beautiful."

Lydia giggled. "Oh, Joe." Then she stopped smiling. "You know, I don't approve of this forced union. I think you two are being railroaded into this marriage, but I can't really fault the reverend for his judgment either." She shrugged. "So, I guess you are stuck."

"I appreciate your opinion, Lydia, but I won't risk Hannah's reputation. If I do, she won't have customers for her business in Oregon City. We have no choice." He tipped his hat and walked over to Hannah then smiled. "How are you this morning?"

Nausea threatened to make her vomit, but she was sure the sensation was caused by nerves. "As good as can be expected under the circumstances."

"Everything will work out. I'll just retire sooner than I planned."

She rested a hand on his forearm. "I don't want you to quit because of me. Don't you understand? I never wanted us to marry this way."

His eyes narrowed. "I hadn't planned on being forced to marry either, but we have to deal with the consequences of our actions."

Hannah nodded and then threw up her hands. "All we did was kiss. It's not like we were," her voice dropped to almost a whisper. "Fornicating for the whole world to see. I just want you to know that I didn't kiss you just so this marriage would happen. I kissed you because I wanted to. I have for weeks."

Joe pushed a loose strand of hair behind her ear, took both her hands in his and kissed the top of each one. "I wanted to kiss you, too. We'll do the best we can." Then he leaned close. "There will be no annulment. You and I will be man and wife and I intend to make you my wife in all ways."

Hannah's eyes widened. "You can't mean to… to…well, you know. Here? Everyone will hear."

He smiled. "I've arranged for us to stay in the fort's guest quarters. We'll arrive there at about noon. I rode there and back last night. The colonel in charge is an old friend."

Hannah didn't know whether to be relieved or terrified. She went with terrified. Not only were events moving way too fast, her mother had never gotten around to explaining to her and Lydia about wedding nights. Oh, she had a general idea, but no idea if what her married friends told her was true or not.

"Shouldn't we wait until we get to know each other better? I mean, we've only known each other for a couple of months."

"And I've eaten breakfast and dinner with you and Lydia almost every day for the last month. Everyone figured this would be the outcome. They figured I was courting you."

"What? You were what?"

Joe frowned and slowly shook his head. "In my own way, I guess I was courting you. Don't tell me you thought I spent my time with you for any other reason."

She tilted her head to the side. "Well, I guess I thought you liked my company. I didn't much think about it, but now that I do, your actions make sense for someone courting, and I seem the fool."

Joe stood in front of her. "You're not a fool. You're naïve, that's all. And I like that you don't know everything. You haven't become jaded."

"What will you do about the felons on the wagon train? Do you still plan on turning them in at Fort Laramie?"

"Yes. That means I'll be busy for most of the rest of the morning and maybe the entire day. And, no, you cannot help."

Her chin lifted a notch. "I can handle myself, you know. You just concentrate on the bad guys and I'll see they don't evade you."

"Hannah." He slowly drew out both syllables of her name. "If you could handle yourself, you'd have bought your boots soon enough to get the right size. My line of work doesn't allow for mistakes like that. Ever. Now stay here and out of my way. Please."

She took a deep breath. "I promise."

"And that you'll stay here."

"I promise I'll stay with the wagons unless Lydia needs me elsewhere. I'm supposed to restock our food stores."

"Fine. Just don't put yourself in danger. Understand?"

"I won't put myself in danger."

Joe checked his pocket watch. "We should get going. The reverend will think we changed our minds."

He held his arm for her to take.

She placed her hand into the crook of his elbow.

With Lydia following, they crossed the empty space in the circle of wagons to Reverend Trowbridge's wagon.

He awaited them with the Bible in his hand.

"Very good. I was afraid you young people might have changed your minds."

Joe patted Hannah's hand. "We haven't, Reverend. You can start the ceremony now."

Reverend Trowbridge nodded toward the gray-haired woman who stood slightly to the left and behind him. "My wife, Adela, will act as the second witness. Miss Lydia Granger as the first."

"Let's just get this ceremony over with, shall we?" asked Joe.

Hannah worried that Joe would resent her for the rest of his life, but what else could she do? He was very insistent they marry. *I promise to be the best wife he could ever want. I won't let him regret his decision to marry me rather than walk away.*

Reverend Trowbridge began the ceremony.

"We are gathered together to join this man and this woman in holy matrimony. If anyone knows why this marriage should not take place, speak now or forever hold your peace."

He stopped and raked his gaze over the crowd that was forming.

No one spoke.

"Very good." He turned toward Joe. "Do you Joseph Stanton take this woman, Hannah Granger to be your lawfully wedded wife? To have and to hold, through sickness and health, for richer and for poorer? Do you promise to love and honor her and to keep yourself only unto her, for as long as you both shall live?"

Joe gazed down at Hannah. "I do." He pulled a simple gold band from his vest pocket and placed it on the third finger of her left hand. "It was my mother's," he whispered.

Reverend Trowbridge turned his gaze on Hannah. "Do you Hannah Granger, take this man, Joseph Stanton to be your lawfully wedded husband? To have and to hold, through sickness and health, for richer and for poorer? Do you promise to love, honor and *obey* him, keeping yourself only unto him, for as long as you both shall live?"

Pulse racing and a lump in her throat, she raised her gaze to Joe's smiling face. "I do."

"Then, by the power vested in me by the Lord, God Almighty, I pronounce you husband and wife. You may kiss the bride."

Joe cupped her face with his palms. "With pleasure." He lowered his head and took her lips in a sweet kiss.

When she would have pulled away, he held her fast and kissed her more thoroughly, using his tongue to tease her and to taste her, as she did him.

The crowd clapped.

The noise brought them back to reality and they pulled apart.

Hannah looked down at the gold ring Joe placed on her finger. Then she looked up at him, smiled and took his hand.

He raised her hand, kissed the ring on her finger and squeezed her hand a little.

"Hello, Mrs. Stanton."

"Hello, Mr. Stanton. You're a quite scandalous man giving me a kiss like that, in front of everyone."

"I figured a kiss is what got us into this, we might as well enjoy another."

Lydia approached, hugged Hannah and then Joe. "I made an apple cobbler last night from most of their remaining apples, to celebrate. Come have some before you leave to get back to work."

"We'd be pleased to, Lydia," said Joe. He kept Hannah's hand in his.

Hannah grinned at Lydia and nodded.

She was happier than she'd ever been and yet, she couldn't help fearing that a dark cloud hung over them. The wedding was as nice as it could be in this rural location. Nothing would have made the ceremony better other than not having to have it at all. Hannah still worried that Joe would resent her, even worse, what if she came to resent him?

After eating the cobbler, the wedding celebration was over. Hannah and Lydia changed into their everyday dresses and out of the silk ones.

The wagon train still had to reach Fort Laramie today. They were only a couple of miles outside the fort, but because the oxen were bordering on exhaustion as were the people driving them, the distance would was great enough it would take several hours for them to arrive.

They would stay for a few days at the fort.

Hannah was riding the horse. Lydia drove the wagon and walked because walking was easier on her body than riding in the wagon.

"Lydia. Look." Hannah pointed at buildings visible in the distance. Laramie sat on the high prairie with the mountains not far away. The American flag flew high above the fort.

The wagons formed a circle outside the gates.

Hannah had left the wagon train and rode toward the fort. She was surprised to find the buildings were not of wood but of adobe brick which looked almost like stone. Everyone would be needing their supplies restocked.

She barely made it in time to be first, sliding from the saddle just ahead of Priscilla McCoy, whose wagon was the first in line for this week. Winded and unable to catch her breath in the high altitude, Hannah marched into the store.

A man with brown hair, brown eyes, and a kindly smile stood behind the counter.

"What can I do for you today, little lady?"

"Hello. I'm Hannah Granger...er...Stanton and I'd like to buy supplies, please. Here is my list."

The man took the list and totaled the prices right on the paper.

"This lot will cost thirty-two dollars and fifty cents. If you pay now, I'll have it delivered to you when your wagon pulls up."

My goodness that's twice as much as the cost would be in Independence for the same items, but I won't complain. "That sounds good to me." Hannah pulled off her gloves, removed the money from her reticule and paid for the food. She still had nearly one-hundred seventy dollars from the money Mr. Mosley sent. They had included extra flour, sugar and tinned fruit on the list in case Lydia decided to sell some of her cakes to make money. She bet the soldiers in the fort would like a fresh baked cake or bowl of cobbler. And she'd added more of everything to accommodate Joe at all meals. They didn't really need to make money, but they didn't want to arrive in Oregon City dead broke either. "I'll need a receipt for the groceries."

"Of course. Here you are." He handed her back her list with his signature on the bottom and the total amount paid.

"Great. I'll be back in about thirty minutes to lead your wagon to ours. She stopped and turned back. "Do you have any gold men's wedding rings?"

"All I have are plain gold bands."

"That would be perfect. I don't know what size he needs."

"I'll pick out one and you can bring it back for the right size if it's wrong. How tall is your husband?"

"Six foot three inches.'

"Is he thin or fat?"

"Neither. He's perfect."

The clerk chuckled. "All right I'm giving you an eleven. Like I said if it doesn't fit, bring it back. The price is twenty dollars."

Hannah paid him. "Thank you so much. I really appreciate it." She took the ring putting it in her bag.

"That's fine and I'll be expecting your wagon in about thirty minutes."

Then the man turned his attention to Priscilla. Taking orders would go on for some time, as each of the wagons bought what they could afford. Hannah thought most of the brides and families making up the wagon train were in similar straights as she and Lydia. No rich person crossed the country in a wagon train. They'd sail around the Horn. Sailing was faster and more comfortable...and much more expensive.

Hannah wandered about the fort. In addition to the general store, she saw the barracks, livery, blacksmith shop and several buildings she couldn't identify.

"Well, now, what do we have here? If it isn't Miss Granger. Where is your protector now?"

Hannah knew that voice and whirled to face the man who'd caused her and Joe so much grief. "What are you doing here, Dick Bailey? Aren't you afraid Joe will kill you? Because you should be."

"He won't do nothin' here. He'd be the one arrested. Besides," He held up his right hand covered in a big, thick bandage. "I owe him for this."

"I don't think so. You brought your injury on yourself when you tried to kill Joe. The post commander is a friend of Joe's. Given the circumstances, I don't think he'll arrest Joe at all, though he may arrest you."

The skin between Bailey's eyebrows crinkled, and he frowned. "What would he arrest me for? I ain't done nothin'."

She held up a hand and ticked off the fingers one by one. "How about trying to kill Joe, for one? Pestering Joe's wife for another. I'm sure if they wanted to, they'd find something in your background that you've done and probably have a bounty on your head for."

Bailey's eyes widened. "I ain't done nothin', I tell ya. Nothin' at all."

She stood straighter. Bailey didn't frighten her. "I suggest you leave the fort before Joe sees you."

Joe appeared behind Bailey. He had a frown on his face and his hand hovered over his holster.

"Too late for that, but if he leaves now, I might forget I saw him."

Bailey paled.

"I'm leavin'."

He turned and ran, glancing back at Joe and Hannah before heading in the direction of the livery.

Joe placed his hands on Hannah's shoulders and ran them down her arms. "Are you all right?"

Hannah wrapped her hands around his where they rested on her shoulders. "I'm fine. Really. He didn't touch me. I scared him more than he scared me, especially after I told him we were married."

Joe laughed and let his hands slide down her arms again before dropping them to his sides. "I bet he did. I'm sure he's nursing that hand of his, too."

Hannah nodded, almost unable to speak due to the shivers his touch gave her. " He...ah..." She shook her head to get her mind back to business. "He said he owed you for the injury. I get the feeling if he got the chance to shoot you in the back; he'd take it, so please take care. I'm much too young to be a widow…goodness, I just became a bride."

He grinned. "That you did. Come see the quarters we'll be staying in for as long as the wagon train's here."

He took her arm and tucked her hand into the crook of his elbow. They started across the courtyard toward a large two-story building. He pointed to the room on the lower right corner. "The next room is vacant, as is the one above. That's as much privacy as we can get."

She pressed her hand to her collar and smiled. "That's wonderful. Thank you."

He tilted his head and furrowed his brows. "For what?"

"You didn't need to take my concerns into account. Lots of men wouldn't. Thank you for not being like other men."

His mouth quirked up on one side, and he shook his head slowly. "Thank God, you're not like other women."

She straightened and cocked her head to one side. "You wouldn't have been interested in me if I'd been like other girls."

"True. They're a dime a dozen, but you, you're worth your weight in gold."

Her throat tightened. "Ah, Joe. I think I'm gonna cry."

"No. I forbid it."

Her tears evaporated. "You forbid it? You're actually forbidding me to cry."

Nodding, he folded his arms over his chest. "Yes. I hate tears. Women use them to manipulate men to do their bidding."

She stepped away before she really lost her temper. "We cry for lots of reasons. Maybe we're just sad or happy or whatever."

He shrugged. "Maybe, but that's not been my experience."

"I'm sorry for you. No one should be so bitter at such a young age. I never asked before, though I don't know why, but how old are you anyway?"

"I'm thirty. How old are you?"

"Twenty-three."

"I knew it. You're a youngster."

She put her hands on her hips. "And you're an old man. What of it?"

He grinned, put his thumbs in his pockets and rocked back on his heels. "You're standing up for yourself. You've got spirit...spunk...and I like it. Nothing will ever be boring with you."

She threw up her hands and turned to walk away. "I don't understand you."

Joe caught her with a hand on her arm. "Wait. Don't go away mad. Let's go inside and look at the room we have for the next three nights. Chester says that's how long we'll be here. He wants to give the animals a rest and the people, too. But if we stay any longer we might have to cross the Blue Mountains in snow and crossing them then is not a good thing."

Hannah took a deep breath and let it out. "Okay. Let's see this room."

He took her hand in his.

She looked up at him. Still unable to really believe he was her husband. She loved him so much. The fact she could never tell him hurt. She wanted to shout it to the sky. That wouldn't happen.

He squeezed her hand.

"Aren't you worried people will see us holding hands?"

"Nope."

"But—"

"But what? I'm holding hands with my wife. No one will say anything about that once they know we're married."

"I suppose you're right."

"Are you trying to avoid touching me, wife?"

"No! I mean, yes. Oh, I don't know what I mean." Hannah rolled her eyes in frustration.

"Are you afraid, Hannah?"

She nodded. "Yes. I wouldn't be a good virgin if I wasn't."

He chuckled. "Walk with me while we talk. We'll attract less attention that way. What are you afraid of?"

She shook her head. "Pain. Embarrassment. The normal things a bride fears. What if you don't like what you see? I'm not willowy like Lydia."

Joe smiled. "Anything else?"

She huffed out a breath and tilted her head. "Aren't those enough?"

He didn't smile now. "First, I'll do my best to prepare you, so the pain will be less. After all I'm not a rutting beast. I'm your husband and I don't want to hurt you. Second, I know you're not, what did you call it? Willowy. I like you just like you are. I want a woman who is not skin and bones but is curvy in the right places. I want you."

At the same time, Hannah was terrified and pleased. Picturing Joe seeing her naked was mortifying, but he'd said he wanted a woman with curves and that was certainly her.

Still, she worried. *I love Joe. What if he doesn't ever love me? Can I live in a marriage where I'm the only one in love?*

CHAPTER 8

They walked to the two-story building that housed the bachelor officers. Joe said he colonel told him the building was called Old Bedlam.

They walked up the stairs on the right side of Old Bedlum to a porch that ran the length of the building. There appeared to be twelve rooms, six up and six down. The building itself seemed out of place in the rustic surroundings of Fort Laramie, with it's adobe buildings. Bordered by a white picket fence, with two massive chimneys in the middle of the roof, the two-story building was part wood and part adobe all of which was painted white. Stairs on either side of the balcony gave access to the second-floor rooms.

Joe led them into the room that would be theirs. He held the door for Hannah and closed it behind her when she stepped into the center of the room.

A pretty cotton rug, dark blue with dots of white so it looked like stars in the night sky, covered the center of the floor.

A pretty patchwork quilt was spread across the double sized brass bed with four posts instead of the rounded headboard and footboard. She ignored her thought that the brass bed seemed out of place in a bachelor's room. Maybe she and Joe weren't the only ones they loaned the rooms out to.

"This will be our room for the next few nights."

Hannah felt the heat in her cheeks and knew she was red as a beet.

Joe chuckled. "You'll have to get used to us having relations. Talking about making love, between the two of us, is nothing to be embarrassed about. Husbands and wives need to be able to talk about anything...everything."

Hannah closed her eyes and took a deep breath before opening them. "I know you're right, but discussing fornication seems wrong. I've spent too many years being told, 'No. We don't talk about that.' Now, because we're married, the rules have changed. Give me some time to adapt."

"You can have whatever time you need. Our relationship is an ongoing experiment for both of us. It's been a long time since I was married."

Hannah lifted an eyebrow. "What happened?"

Joe walked to the window and put his hands in his pockets. Then he looked out into the parade ground of the fort. "I was very young, just sixteen.

My girl was only fifteen. We ran away and got married. Figured our folks couldn't say anything then. We were wrong. Her father was the county judge. He had the marriage annulled and sent Sandra off to a boarding school in the East. My parents were just poor dirt farmers, but Sandra hadn't cared. We were going to start our own place. I stayed and worked with my Dad and Sandra was gone to school for two years."

Hannah squeezed Joe's hand. "What happened when she came back?"

"She'd changed and was just like her mother. The snootiest, nastiest girl you'd ever want to meet. She acted like I was beneath her, called me Joseph, refused to even talk again about getting married." He turned to Hannah. "I'd wasted all that time waiting for someone who was gone forever. Oh, the girl was still there, but the sweet person she'd been was gone."

"I'm supposed to say I'm sorry." Hannah looked up at him, his eyes seemed sadder, the crinkles around them deeper. "But I'm not. If you'd married her again, you wouldn't have been free to marry me. Probably wouldn't be a bounty hunter and certainly wouldn't be the person you are now. At least, now I understand why you don't want this marriage annulled."

She lifted a hand to his face and pulled the back of her hand slowly down his cheek. "We'll make this union work. Together."

For a second, he closed his eyes and then opened them, staring at her intently. "I can only give you one piece of advice. Don't fall in love with me because I can't love you back. You'll only be hurt."

She stopped her hand on its journey down his cheek and lowered it to her side. "Don't worry. The chance of that happening is non-existent." Her heart was breaking, but she'd never let him know. *I love you, Joe Stanton, and I'll never tell you. I'll never make you feel guilty for not loving me back.*

He cocked an eyebrow and then nodded. "Good."

Joe turned her around and wrapped his arms around her waist.

"What do you think? Can you manage to stay in such rustic quarters for a few days?"

Hannah chuckled, leaned back into him and rested her arms on top of his. "Oh, I think I'll manage."

He kissed her hair and nuzzled her neck.

Almost without thought, she tilted her head to the side to give him greater access to her throat.

Joe turned her in his arms until she faced him. Then he leaned down and kissed her. He unbuttoned the top fastening of her dress and then the next and the next.

Then she registered what was happening.

Gasping, she stepped back and swatted at his hands, refastening the buttons he'd undone.

"What are you doing? We can't do anything now."

"Why not? No one will miss either of us for hours."

He lifted his hands to her dress.

She covered his hands with hers. "Joe, rushing through the act isn't how I want to give myself to you. I don't want to have to hurry or worry that someone will knock on the door needing us for some reason. Please, let's wait until tonight."

Joe stilled and dropped his arms to his sides before clasping her hands in his.

"You're right. I don't know what I was thinking. I don't want to have to hurry either. Roger wants us to come to dinner in about an hour and that is definitely not enough time. I just want you so much and now that you're my wife, I can make love to you any time I want. The knowledge went right to my head and I didn't think any farther. Tonight, maybe after a walk under the stars and a glass of wine to relax you, then we'll consummate our vows."

"Those things sound wonderful and more what I had in mind for my first time."

Hannah did her best not to show her fear. She loved Joe and was sure he wouldn't hurt her on purpose. He'd said he'd never love her but she didn't accept those words as fact. She couldn't. Because having a marriage based on friendship wasn't enough for her. But she was also sure he'd love her someday. He just had to.

"Hannah? Are you all right?"

Joe waved a hand in front of her face.

"Hannah?"

She blinked her eyes and shook her head, ridding her mind of its troubling thoughts.

"I'm sorry. I was picturing this room, well, not this actual room, but one like it, in our new home in Oregon City." She wrapped her arms around him and lifted onto tiptoe to kiss him.

"Independence," he whispered against her lips.

She pulled back like she'd been struck by lightning. *He can't be serious.*

"No. Not Independence. Oregon City."

"Why? What difference does it make as long as we're together? Independence is bigger and closer to my work."

"You can work anywhere you want. If you couldn't, you'd have a home already somewhere. And since you won't allow me to come with you, I want to be near Lydia while you're gone."

For a moment he was silent.

Hannah was afraid maybe she'd overstepped her bounds.

Then his lips curved up and he nodded.

"Yup. Spunk. I like it. We'll live in Oregon City while I finish up with my bounties."

She tilted her head just a little. "That's another thing. I don't want you to quit your work because of me. I want to help you."

"No."

"But I see things you don't...like that man on the wagon train."

He shook his head. "I don't want to worry about you and have to protect you."

"Then teach me how to shoot better so I can protect myself."

Joe crossed his arms over his chest. "No."

"Do you know any other word besides 'no'?"

He grinned. "Yes."

Hannah rolled her eyes toward the ceiling and took a deep breath. *No use arguing with the man.*

"Fine." She turned toward the door.

Joe reached out and wrapped her in his arms, pulling her back against his chest. "I know what that word means. You are anything but fine. Talk to me, Hannah."

She struggled, weakly. In actuality, she loved having his arms around her. "All right, let's talk. Neither you nor I are happy that we had to marry the way we did, but we are both determined to make the best of it, now that I know you don't want an annulment. So why can't I help you? Why are you determined to leave me home while you go off chasing bad guys?" *I'm fully capable of helping him. I can shoot a rifle, I can cook for him and we can keep each other company, too.*

He kissed the top of her head.

"You think what I do is easy and we'll catch the criminals easily. Catching them quickly or easily doesn't happen. The one time it has turned out that way is this time. Colonel Travers has agreed to send half a dozen soldiers with me to apprehend the three men on the wagon train. But this is a very unusual situation. Arresting the bad men and getting the bounties has never happened so quickly. Travers will send them back to Independence with an armed escort. They will return with the money for the bounties. He'll send me the money in Oregon City with the next wagon train that comes through."

"So why aren't they all that easy? You find the wanted man and turn him in." She snapped her fingers. "Why is it so hard?"

He kissed her neck, nipped her gently with his teeth and then soothed the nip with his tongue and another kiss.

"I may ride for days without seeing another soul. Finding them can take months and then they'll do everything they can to escape once I have them. I have to be on guard at all times. Never let their sad stories affect me. I sleep rough, usually on the ground under the stars. It's not romantic, it's hard and cold."

"But I could keep you warm...I—"

He spun her in his arms so she faced him.

"Hannah. No. You can't come with me. How many times do I have to say it?"

Joe let her go and turned away. He threw his hat on the bed and ran his hands through his hair.

"Why are you making this situation so hard?"

Hannah closed her eyes. "I'm not trying to make anything hard. I'm trying to find a way to spend time with my husband and maybe have an adventure, too. I admit it. What you do intrigues me."

"I'm quitting. It's not an adventure. It's work and hard with long days in the saddle. It's dangerous. I don't know when someone I'm chasing will decide to shoot me in the back. It wouldn't be the first time."

Hannah's eyes widened and her hand flew to her throat. "You've been shot? When? Where?"

He shrugged and pointed to the spots he'd taken a bullet. "The back, left arm, in the right leg, twice."

"Oh, my God. Joe, I had no idea. I—"

"You romanticized the job in your mind. You thought it would be fun and games. It's not. When will you get the reality through your head?"

Hannah clasped her hands in front of her and looked at the floor, anywhere but at him. "You're right. I did think it would be fun. I didn't think about what could happen. I'm sorry."

"Good." He grabbed his hat from the bed. "Let's go. I suddenly don't feel like making love."

Joe opened the door and stood, silhouetted in the opening with the sun behind him.

"Are you coming?"

Nodding she hurried out the door. She didn't stop walking to wait for him, just kept her head down and put one foot in front of the other, heading back to the wagon train. How could she have been so stupid?

Joe caught up with her just as she stepped off the stairs and onto the path. He opened the gate in the picket fence for her and shut it after her.

Hannah didn't slow.

For a few steps, he walked beside her before taking her arm and stopping her.

"Hannah? What's the matter now?"

When she looked up at him, the tears filling her eyes escaped and rolled down her cheeks. "I'm so stupid. I'm sorry, Joe. If you weren't regretting this marriage before, I'm sure you do now. I've been acting like a child, not listening to what you were trying so hard to tell me."

Joe took her hand, brought it to his lips and kissed it.

"You're not stupid. You're a romantic and I don't want you to become cynical either. I want you to be amazed when you see the ocean for the first time and maybe every time after. I like that you want to be with me, but that doesn't mean I won't stop you when you want to come with me. Understand?"

She's glad to hear his calm tone. "I do now. I really do."

"Good. Let's go see if the store has your supplies loaded in their wagon. I'll drive the wagon and you bring the horses."

"I've never led a horse before. How about we tie the horses behind the buckboard and both ride in the wagon?"

"Okay. That solution works, too."

Hannah smiled. Her heart was lighter. She felt like they had a chance at a happy marriage. Joe cared for her and that fact was a good beginning. All she had to do was make sure she was irresistible enough he couldn't help but fall in love with her.

But how could she become irresistible?

CHAPTER 9

The supplies were ready. Joe and Hannah took them out to the wagon train.

"Lydia," called Hannah as they arrived at the wagon. "Lydia, we're back."

Lydia came around the back of the wagon. The front of her dress was smeared with blood. She carried something in her hands which were red with blood.

What in the world happened?

"Lydia!" Hannah jumped off the buckboard and ran to her sister as Joe drew the horses to a stop. "What happened? Are you all right? Why are you covered in blood?"

Lydia giggled. "Yes, I'm fine, but this little one's mama is not. She's very weak and I don't think she'll live much longer."

Joe came up to them and pointed at the animal

in Lydia's arms. "That's a mountain lion cub, you know. Right?"

"Of course, but he needs help." She looked over at Joe. "He's the only surviving cub from a litter of three and his mama will likely not make it through the night, despite my efforts. He needs our help."

"How did you find them?" asked Joe.

"I went down to the river and heard moaning in the tall grass near the water. She was trying to get to the water for a drink and was too weak to even crawl there. I took off my shoe and filled it then took it back to her. At first, she growled at me but when I dribbled water on her, she let me come closer."

Joe ran his hand behind his neck. "She let you come closer!" He yelled. "Are you crazy? You could have been mauled or killed."

With a single shake of her head, she dismissed the thought. "Nonsense. She wasn't capable of either action. Now, I need to clean up this little guy and then let him nurse for as long as she lives."

Lydia grabbed a bucket and poured in water from the water barrel. Then she took a washcloth, a towel, her rose-scented soap and headed to the river with the tiny newborn cub.

As he watched her go, Joe shook his head. "She's going to get her heart broken. That little cat won't survive without its mother."

Hannah smiled. "You've never seen Lydia when an animal needs her help. The kitten and the wolf cub were nothing. She'll nurse this little one with milk until he's old enough for solid food and then she'll have them all joining us for supper. You wait and see."

Joe shook his head. "What will she do with that cat when he gets full grown? Keep him as a pet?"

"Yes, she probably will. By that time, he'll be too used to people to return to the wild, even if she could get him to go. He'll believe Lydia is his mother, and he won't want to leave her."

"Well, make sure she keeps him under wraps for as long as possible. There'll be uproar on the wagon train if they find out she's got a lion cub."

"We'll keep him quiet. Trinity and Sampson are doing just fine in that department. We've had no complaints."

He looked around. "Sampson?"

"That's what she named the wolf pup."

"Why Sampson?"

Hannah shrugged. "She just liked the name. He's the strong man from the Bible and Lydia says the wolf will be strong, too."

Joe rolled his eyes. "Of course, I should have known."

She laughed. "No, you shouldn't. The selection of the name makes sense only to Lydia."

Lydia returned half an hour later with the lion cub. He was meowing, actually yowling was more accurate.

She walked over to them, her eyes filled with tears. "His mama is dead."

Hannah wrapped her arms around her sister, unmindful of the bloody dress or the cub in her arms. She hugged her until the little cat yowled loudly.

She and Lydia parted and the cub seemed satisfied. He relaxed in Lydia's arms and actually purred.

Hannah chuckled. "He's already accepted you as his mama. How will you feed him?"

"I'll use an eye dropper at first, and then I'll soak a washcloth in milk to let him suck on it until he learns to lap liquids into his mouth."

"I'll help you. He'll need to be fed all the time."

Joe walked up and scratched the cub's head. "He is a cute little thing now that he's clean and dry. I'm sorry about his mama. It's unusual for a puma to be down this low. They're mostly found in the mountains west of here."

"She'd been shot and must have come down here to give birth. That's the only thing I can think of," said Lydia.

When the baby cat hissed at him, Joe smiled. "Yup, definitely a cougar."

Hannah's brows wrinkled. "You've used at least three different names for this animal." She ticked them off with her fingers. "Mountain lion, puma, and now cougar. Any more names for him?"

Joe nodded but continued to scratch the little cat's ears. "Yes, they're also called catamounts and panthers as is the black jaguar."

"Oh, my." She looked at Lydia. "I guess you'd better give this little guy a name so we can all call him the same thing."

Lydia smiled and held up the baby with her hands around his chest and his body hanging. "I'm calling him Simba, because he'll be big and strong, just like a lion, when he grows up. But he'll be a good kitty. Isn't that right? Yes, you will." She nuzzled the cub's tummy and then kissed his nose before enveloping him in her arms once again.

Joe lifted an eyebrow and then looked toward the sky. "I've never heard such a name. It sounds foreign."

Hannah smiled. She knew how Lydia's mind worked.

"Because Simba is Swahili for lion. She's read a few articles about the travels of Dr. David Livingstone in Africa."

"So we have Trinity, the three-legged cat," Joe counted the names with his fingers. "Sampson, the wolf pup, and now Simba, a panther cub. Is this the end of the animals? Please tell me it's the end of the animals."

Hannah nodded and then grinned. "Until the next foundling, she picks up. Since she was a little girl she's always brought home stray and wounded animals. Drove our parents crazy, but she always took care of them and never let them get in anyone's way. Though this is the first time for a wolf and a cougar."

"What if Lydia has children? How will the animals get along with a real baby? And what is her mail-order husband going to say about her little menagerie?"

"I don't know. But we probably will find out at some point in time. I don't see her remaining childless forever."

"What about when we have children. You do want children, don't you?"

"I do. What about you?" She reflected on the fact that Joe wanted kids. She couldn't believe her luck in finding a man she loves and one who wants children, too.

He nodded. "Now that being a father is a real possibility, I find I like the idea."

She reflected on the fact that Joe wanted kids. She couldn't believe her luck in finding a man she loves and one who wants children, too.

"What I don't like is those wild animals." He jutted his chin toward Lydia and her menagerie. "I don't want our children exposed to her wild animals. They shouldn't be made pets."

Hannah put fisted hands on her hips. "When will I, or our children get to see her, if you forbid it? Assuming I decide to abide by your rules."

"She can come to see us, and then there is no danger to our kids."

She glared at him. "Do you honestly think I would put our children at risk? That I would go to Lydia's home if I didn't believe it was perfectly safe to do so?" Hannah pointed at Joe. "Seems we have a lot to learn about each other...before we make love."

Joe ran a hand over the back of his neck. "Look, Hannah, we're talking about having children. We know we're staying married and besides, the best way to know someone is when they are naked. You can't hide anything then. If you don't want to make love, I won't force you, but I think we should still take the room. I don't know about you, but I could use a real bed for a few nights."

"Does it cost us money for the room?"

"No. Roger...Colonel Travers is giving it to us as a wedding gift."

She gazed at him. His exhaustion was unmistakable for anyone really looking at him. Dark circles were under his eyes, the crinkles around his mouth and at the corner of his eyes more prominent and he didn't fight with her like he usually did. Her heart ached for the pain she caused him. Hannah wondered if she was fighting with him because she was afraid of intimacy or if she really felt he was being a bully. She knew the answer but didn't want to face it.

I'm afraid. Afraid of the pain. Afraid I'll be bad at making love. What if I am and he decides to find someone else?

"Yes, I guess we both could. You look tired, exhausted actually. I hope the few days of rest will rejuvenate you."

"I know it can't hurt."

He scrubbed both hands over his face.

The gesture only served to make him look more tired.

"You don't have to be at the wagon train for anything so let's leave. You can rest when we get back to the room."

"Only if you let me hold you."

Heat filled her cheeks and she couldn't believe her ears. "Ho...hold me?" *Why would he want to hold me?*

He grinned and lifted an eyebrow. "Yup. Hold you. You're my wife and I won't make love to you until you're ready but I want to hold you and pretend you want me as much as I want you."

With just his words, Joe managed to keep her color high. She didn't think she'd ever be normal again.

After they dropped off the buckboard at the fort's store, they walked down to Old Bedlam and into the room that would be theirs for the next three nights.

Now that she looked at the room with something other than fear, she realized it was really quite nice. Across from the brass bed was a long, light-colored wood dresser with six drawers, three on either side. A comfortable looking, over-stuffed chair sat beneath the window for reading. On the wall next to the door was a chest of drawers, and a nightstand stood on either side of the bed.

All of the furniture was designed with clean lines and definitely a man in mind.

She remembered her mother helping her father off with his boots and thought the gesture the right thing to do. "Do you need help with your boots?"

Joe grinned. "I think I can handle them."

Hannah backed up a couple of steps. "Of course, you can. Forgive me."

"Nothing to forgive. I like that you want to help me."

He removed his gun belt and hung it on the headboard. Then he unbuttoned his shirt and slid it off his arms.

Hannah looked at Joe's body. She knew she should look away, but for the life of her, she couldn't. He was beautiful, for lack of a better word. His arms and chest looked as though sculpted from marble.

Joe unbuttoned his pants.

Finally Hannah looked away. "What are you doing?"

"I'm getting comfortable. Why?"

"Oh. Let me know when you're under the blankets."

"Hannah."

He sounded tired.

"I won't hurt you and you have to get used to me. You might as well start now."

She paused and then nodded. "You're right. I need to stop being a child." She straightened her spine and threw back her shoulders. She looked down at her clasped hands and then up at him. "I'm ready when you are."

Joe shook his head and stopped taking off his pants. He sat on the side of the bed and took off his boots, then he laid back on the mattress, his head on the pillow. He held out his arm.

"Come here."

Hannah didn't hesitate this time. She went around the bed to the other side, removed her boots, then crawled over to him. There she nestled into his side and his arm came around her.

"This is better, don't you think?"

"Yes." As much as she didn't want to admit he was right, he actually was. He pulled her close and whispered. "In my arms is where you belong."

He was asleep in no time.

Hannah, on the other hand, lay awake for what seemed like hours. Being next to Joe was comfortable, more so that she'd ever imagined and she settled against him.

As she did, his arm tightened around her and she wondered if he was awake, but his snores convinced her he slept.

Light from the morning sun washed the bedroom with soft orange and gold. The sight was beautiful but Hannah was too tired to enjoy the scene. She was so warm and comfortable. She cuddled into the warmth then realized Joe was keeping her warm. She stiffened and Joe rubbed her arm until she relaxed again. He pulled her closer, which seemed impossible, and yet he did it. She was tucked safely into his side.

He kissed the top of her head. "Lying together is the way we should always be. No matter what happens, we don't go to bed angry. I always want you in my arms."

She relaxed against him, her head on his shoulder and an arm across his chest. "All right. I can agree to not going to bed angry. I want to be able to sleep and I did that more last night than I would have thought possible. I'm surprised we slept all night. We missed dinner. Lydia is probably worried."

"I know. I slept well, too. We were exhausted. I'm not surprised we slept for more than twelve hours."

Hannah sighed. "I need to get up. I have to help Lydia with the morning chores."

"Are you sure?"

"Yes. I told her I would. There's a lot for one person to do and I want to make sure she knows we're okay."

"All right." He released her by straightening his arm.

She rolled away from him to the edge of the bed. She put on her boots and then walked over to the bureau and looked into the mirror above it.

"Oh, my." Hannah ran a hand over her hair. "This is a disaster and I don't have my brush." She took the thick, red mass out of the bun at the nape of her neck and let it loose down her back. Running her fingers through it, removing as many tangles as possible. Hannah got her hair as tidy as she could get it without a brush.

"You look beautiful. I love your hair down."

"If it wasn't so windy, I might leave it down, but I can't. The weather is much too hot. I have to get it off my neck and besides it would be so full of knots by the end of the day I'd probably have to cut it."

"We don't want you to do that, but you could wear it down at night, couldn't you?"

"I suppose I could if doing so would make you happy."

"It would."

She smiled and wound her hair around and around until it formed a bun at the back of her head. Securing it with pins, then looking in the mirror, she was satisfied that was the best she could do.

"Come for breakfast when you're dressed."

"I will."

Hannah walked out, closing the door behind her and wondered if she should have kissed Joe goodbye. She hurried across the fort grounds and to the wagon train outside. As soon as she cleared the gate, she stopped dead. There were teepees on two sides of the wagon train. During the night the Indians had set up their camp.

She'd read about the homes the Indians had. Called teepees, they were conical in shape, formed by long poles tied together at the top and then covered with animal hides. The hides were usually decorated by the family, depicting hunting scenes and other parts of the family's life. There were at least thirty of the dwellings.

A young soldier, with light blond hair and a gentle demeanor, passed her from the direction of the wagon train.

"Excuse me, sir."

The man took off his hat. "Oh, I'm not a sir, ma'am. I'm just a private. Private Munson."

She pointed at the teepees. "Okay, Private Munson, when did the Indians come and what tribe are they?"

"They came just after dark last night. They are part of the Arapaho tribe, ma'am."

Hannah put a hand at her throat. "I take it they are not hostile."

"Oh, no ma'am. Chief Running Fox and his people come every three or four months for trade with the fort."

"I see. Thank you."

"Would you like me to escort you to your wagon?"

"Well, I—"

"That won't be necessary, Private. I'll escort my wife."

"Yes, sir, Mr. Stanton. I didn't know the lady was your wife. Excuse me."

Private Munson hurried off.

Joe held out his arm to Hannah.

She smiled and took it with both hands.

"You're faster than I thought you'd be."

"I can see that. Shall we both go help Lydia?"

"Yes. The chores will go much faster. Do you have to check in with Mr. Gunn?"

"Not until tomorrow."

When they arrived at the wagon, Lydia was sitting on a bucket, feeding the tiny cub. He didn't have his eyes open yet and mewed pitifully whenever she took the eyedropper away to fill it with milk so he could eat again. Trinity and Sampson were on either side of her, eating something from tin plates.

She looked up at their approach.

"Oh, I'm so glad you came early. I wasn't surprised you didn't return for dinner. I know you were both exhausted. We all are. The trip has been arduous. Unfortunately, the only chore I've been able to do is milk the cow. Trying to feed these babies has taken up all my time."

Hannah bent down and kissed her cheek.

Joe kissed her on the other side.

"Don't worry. We'll take care of it," said Joe. "I'll gather the cows and feed them."

"And I'll fix breakfast. With fresh supplies, we'll have scrambled eggs this morning."

Joe winked at Hannah. "Sounds great. Who knew my wife could cook."

"Oh, you! You've had my cooking before." If she'd had a pan in her hand she'd probably have thrown it at him.

He cocked an eyebrow and stroked his chin. "Have I? I thought Lydia did all the cooking."

"Well, that's sort of true. She does most of the cooking, but I know I've...well, I think I've..." Hannah cocked her head to one side. "Maybe I haven't cooked for you. I did for Mr. Titus before we left Independence. Oh well, I am doing breakfast if we get the chores done." She looked at Lydia. "When will Simba be done eating?"

Joe narrowed his eyes. "Who is Mr. Titus? Should I be jealous?"

Hannah and Lydia both laughed. "He's the man who outfitted us, taught us to shoot the rifles and generally took care of us before the trip. He's at least sixty if he's a day."

Joe rolled his neck. "Well, I'm glad I don't have to fight for you this morning. My neck is a little stiff. Not used to having a pillow I guess."

"Simba's very hungry and doesn't show signs of stopping any time soon. If I didn't know better I'd think he'd been starved."

Lydia filled the dropper again and slowly squeezed the milk into the cub's mouth. As soon as she took it away he mewed again.

Hannah jutted her chin toward Simba. "I doubt he knows when he's full."

"You're probably right. I think I'll just give him this half cup of milk and stop. He's little enough, that should fill him up. He'll probably still yowl, because he doesn't know he's full, but as his mama, I need to take care of him and let him be unhappy if need be."

Joe smiled. "You make a good mama."

Lydia blushed, dipped her head toward the cub and then looked up. "Thanks. I do try to do what is best for my animals."

"Why didn't you have any normal pets with you on this journey?" asked Joe.

"I didn't think it would be fair to make them endure the hardships, so I found them homes before I left."

"How many animals are we talking here?"

Hannah got out the cooking pots and pans. "She had six cats, three dogs, a raccoon, and a piglet. Some were harder to find homes for than others. Almost no one wanted the raccoon."

Joe rolled his eyes. "Good grief. I hope you don't end up with that many before we reach Oregon City. Do you know how your fiancé feels about pets?"

"Not directly. I did mention I had some pets, but I didn't tell him how many or what kind."

Joe lifted an eyebrow. "That's a little devious don't you think?"

Lydia shrugged. "Perhaps, but to my credit, he won't have to put up with as many now. Look we've come..." She wrinkled her brows. "How far have we come?"

"We're about a third of the way," answered Joe.

"See and I've only gotten three animals."

Joe shook his head. "Only three, does that mean you'll have nine by the time we reach Oregon City?"

Lydia gave him a sly smile. "Maybe."

Hannah listened to the exchange between her husband and her sister. She had to smile. Poor Joe. He didn't know what he'd gotten himself into by marrying her. Perhaps she should enlighten him. Or not.

CHAPTER 10

The night before was the Fourth of July. It was celebrated at Fort Laramie in grand style. The soldiers and the brides from the train attended or participated in horse races, egg-in-spoon races and three-legged races. That evening, a dance was held, and the brides danced with the soldiers in the fort. Hannah saw several of the couples walking hand-in-hand and was sure some of the men and women, lost their hearts that night.

Many of the women baked pies and cakes which the officers of the fort judged. Lydia won first prize for her apple pie, made from the last of the apples from home. The prize for first place was a five-pound bag of coffee.

Hannah could hardly believe their luck. Five pounds of coffee. That was like having a sack of gold. They could have a fresh pot nearly every day.

They wouldn't, of course. Throwing out perfectly good coffee, just to have a fresh pot, would be wasteful and if there was one thing the Granger girls were not, it was wasteful.

After he'd finished eating breakfast, Joe stood.

"It's time I check in with Chester. Will you ladies be all right until I return?"

Hannah shook her head and rolled her eyes. "Of course. We were okay before you came and we can take care of ourselves."

Joe crossed both his arms over his chest and lifted an eyebrow.

"All right. Things are definitely easier since you joined our party and we appreciate all you've done for us." Hannah stood and crossed both her arms over her chest. "But we don't want to be a burden on you either."

He stepped forward and put his arms around Hannah's waist.

She unfolded her arms and wrapped them around his neck.

Leaning down, he whispered in her ear. "I just want to make sure you're safe."

She leaned back in his arms, sure he would hold her, and ran her knuckles down his cheek. "We are. No one will harm us here outside Fort Laramie." She lowered her voice. "What about your bounties for Mr.'s Smith, Jones, and O'Toole, as they are known here on the wagon train?"

"They are being picked up as we speak."

A soldier galloped up and had his horse skid to a stop next to Joe.

"Mr. Stanton, Colonel Travers would like to see you. Immediately, sir. I'm to give you my horse."

Frowning Joe turned to Hannah. "I'll be back shortly. If I'm not and the train decides to leave, go with the wagon train. I'll catch up."

Hannah nodded. "All right. I thought we'd be here for three days."

"If I'm not mistaken, that won't happen now and you'll pull out before noon, today. You won't make many miles, but you'll be headed out and that's more important."

"Then I'll see you when I see you."

Joe took her in his arms and kissed her soundly.

Hannah was dazed when he let her go.

He turned, hurried to the soldier's horse and swung up into the saddle. He walked the animal until they were safely outside the circle of wagons, then kicked the horse into a gallop, headed for the fort.

The horse skidded to a halt outside the commander's office. Joe slid from the animal and looped the reins around the hitching rail, before hurrying inside.

The sergeant opened the door for Joe.

"What's the matter, Roger?" The colonel, a man with brown hair, graying at the sides and a full beard and mustache, sat behind a heavy oak desk. He stood as Joe entered the room.

He pointed at the chair in front of the desk. "You better sit down."

"I'd rather stand."

"When my men went to get Smith, Jones, and O'Toole from the stockade, all three were gone. I don't know if they left together or separately. From what you told me, I would guess Smith and Jones left together and O'Toole on his own. If that's the case then O'Toole shouldn't be hard to catch. He won't have anyone else to depend on and these mountains are not kind to the uninformed."

Joe finally sat in the leather chair. "Don't I know it? I nearly died my first year out."

The colonel returned to his chair. "I remember. You were damn lucky my men and I were hunting for fresh meat."

"I was."

"I hear you got married."

Joe stiffened, waiting for the ribbing to come. And he continued to wait. "Yes, her name is Hannah. You're not teasing me? I thought we had a pact that neither of us would marry."

"We did but since you're already married, it's all right that I have a fiancée who will arrive with the next wagon train."

Joe burst into laughter. When he stopped, a grin remained on his face. "What would you have done if I hadn't already married?"

"I don't know." Roger shrugged. "I hadn't thought that far ahead. Too many other things on my mind."

Joe nodded. "Can we talk to the guard?"

"He's been waiting until you were ready." Roger frowned. "He's a private and definitely won't ever be anything else in this man's army."

The sergeant just outside the office door came to attention and saluted as Roger passed. Every man they passed did the same thing.

Joe couldn't help but think about the bounties. For all three men the amount would have been twelve-hundred dollars and he could have retired. Now, he was still short of his goal.

Finally, they reached the stockade. Roger led the way inside.

"Is there a good way to interrogate this man?" asked Joe.

"Straight on. It's the only way."

"I'll follow your lead."

Roger nodded and opened the door.

He approached the cell. "Private Bartholomew."

The man jumped to attention and saluted. "Colonel Travers, sir."

They spoke to the man through the cell's bars.

"At ease, soldier. Why did you let the prisoners go? What did they promise you?"

The private relaxed his stance and laced his fingers behind him. "I didn't have any choice. They said they'd kill me if I didn't release them."

Joe rolled his eyes. No one could be that naïve, could he?

Roger released a long breath and shook his head. "Private, did they say how and when they would kill you? They were behind bars and had no weapons."

The privates eyes widened. "They said they would escape when they were transferred and they'd kill me before they left."

"And you believed them?"

"Oh, yes, sir. Was I wrong?"

"Yes, private, you were wrong and now you're the one in trouble. The army will likely put you in prison for releasing the prisoners, but that's not my decision to make."

The private walked to the bunk, sat and put his face in his hands.

"Why am I so stupid? Why?" He smacked his head and berated himself for as long as they stood there. Finally, Joe and the colonel left.

"What will you do now?" Roger asked as they walked back to his office.

"I'll have to track them again. They can't be too far ahead."

"What about your new wife?"

Joe groaned. "Telling her will be difficult. She wants to come with me."

"That wouldn't be a good idea."

Joe threw his hands in the air. "You think I don't know that? In a way, I'm lucky to leave her with her sister. If we'd already made it to Oregon City, I don't know that I could stop Hannah. As it is, she won't abandon Lydia to fend for herself and her feeling responsible for her little sister is good for me."

"When are you leaving?"

Joe glanced at the sun. "Just as soon as I get packed and my horse saddled. I need to take advantage of the light for the next five or so hours"

"I've got an extra horse you can take so you'll make better time. As a matter of fact, take the one you rode in on. Just bring back the saddle and of course, my soldier."

"Thanks, Roger. I really appreciate your help. Now I've got to explain this situation to Hannah."

Joe rode slowly back to the wagon, thinking the entire way about what he would say to his wife. They still hadn't consummated their marriage and they wouldn't until he returned. Would she wait for him? She could always change her mind and get the marriage annulled.

He tied the horse to the back of the wagon and crossed over into the circle. Hannah was doing the dishes and had scraped the leftover food into a tin plate for the kitten and wolf pup. Those two seemed to always be eating.

"Hannah. Can the dishes wait? I need to talk to you."

She picked up a dish towel and dried her hands.

"You look like you've got bad news, so let's have it."

"Smith, Jones, and O'Toole all escaped. Some idiot private let them go when they threatened to kill him."

"Weren't they in jail cells?"

"Yes."

"Then why?"

Joe shook his head. "Just a simple country boy who believed everything he was told."

"I'm sorry. All that work for nothing. I'm assuming the fugitives will try to get away from here as quickly as possible. Or should I be worried?"

"I'm fairly sure they are headed west and I have to go after them before the trail gets cold."

"I need to stay with Lydia."

"Yes." He took off his hat and ran his hand through his hair. "That's not the only reason you can't go. We've talked about this situation. I haven't changed my mind. I can't have you along with me. The circumstance is too dangerous for you and for me."

"You? How do you figure?"

"Because I'll be too worried about you to do my job efficiently."

"But—"

He shook his head. "No buts. This is the way it has to be."

Hannah closed her eyes.

But he saw that she didn't want to give up. She wanted to fight even though it was a losing proposition.

Joe wrapped her in his arms. "Hannah, don't argue about this. You know it has to be this way."

She gazed up at him. "I know you're right, but I hate it. If I didn't need to be with Lydia, I'd argue more. But I know where my responsibilities lie. Here…with Lydia. Not with you."

"That's right. I'll be back as soon as I can." He lowered his chin and spoke softly. "We have some unfinished business that I intend to finish. Will you wait for me?"

"Of course. Why wouldn't I?"

"We haven't consummated our marriage and you might find someone you love."

Hannah lifted a hand to his cheek. "That won't happen. I guarantee it."

He leaned into her hand, then turned and kissed her palm.

Finally, he pulled back and grinned.

"You're quite the passionate little thing, Mrs. Stanton."

"I only learn from the best. You. You've given me my first and only kisses, so whatever I do will be something you've taught me."

He tweaked her nose. "And that's the way it

should be. Now, I have to go. The longer I delay, the colder the trail gets."

"I know. Please be careful. Come back to me, Joe Stanton."

He smiled. "I will, Hannah Stanton. I most definitely will. You stay close to the wagon train at night. If you absolutely have to go to the river, take the rifle with you and don't be afraid to use it. Okay?"

She nodded. "Okay."

Joe let her go and swung into the saddle.

The soldier waited on his horse. They returned to the fort and Joe left the soldier and saddle. He picked up supplies for a couple of months. Hardtack, coffee, jerky, and biscuit makings. That was it. He traveled light.

Once he cleared the fort, he pressed his horse into a gallop. Heading west based on the accounts of two soldiers who'd seen them leave. West toward the mountains. After about ten miles, he turned away from the wagon trail and known roads. He looked for tracks. After an hour or so he found what he was searching for. Three horses going the same way, trying not to be seen since it looked like the tracks were slightly brushed over. But their tracks would be easy for him to find. Three horses, one with a notch in his shoe. He followed them for about five miles when one of the horses, the one with the notch, turned back toward the wagon train.

What was he doing?

Then the answer hit him like a cold bucket of water. He turned around and let his horse have his head. Running for home, as it were.

Joe had to get back to Hannah. He knew clear down to his bones she was in danger. Now that she was his wife, she would always be in danger if he kept up this line of work.

He had two choices—give up tracking bounties or let Hannah go.

Hannah bent over the stream and filled the metal bucket with water. She took her washrag and wet it from the liquid in the bucket. Then she stood and scrubbed her face with the cold cloth.

Suddenly an arm snaked around her neck and pulled her back causing her to lose her balance and lean against the man. His other hand covered her mouth before she could scream.

"Hi, Miss Granger. Or should I say, Mrs. Stanton? It doesn't matter. What matters is you're important to Joe and I want him off my trail."

She bit the fleshy part of his palm covering her mouth.

He shouted and pushed her away.

"You think to kidnap me? Think again. That's not too smart Mr. O'Toole. Joe will never stop looking for me. You have to know that."

CYNTHIA WOOLF

He smiled and Hannah thought he looked like the devil, then he sent his fist into her jaw, sending her sprawling on the ground. Then he pulled his gun.

"You'll do exactly what I say or I'll kill Joe now. Oh, I intend to kill him as soon as he tries to rescue you. I'll shoot him in the back if I can."

"Now hold out your hands. Cross your wrists."

She looked around for the rifle and saw it behind him. "No."

O'Toole stepped forward and raised his gun to pistol whip her.

She plowed into his middle, sending them both to the ground, then she rolled toward the rifle.

Just as she wrapped her hand around it, he stepped on her hand.

"I'll take that. You're a lot feistier than I thought. But now you'll do as you're told or I'll beat you unconscious and throw you over the saddle. One way or another you're coming with me. Understand?"

"Yes."

"Now hold out your hands."

She did as she was told. She had the coppery taste of blood in her mouth. She wouldn't be surprised to find a couple of loose teeth.

O'Toole put a noose around her wrists and pulled it tight, almost too tight.

"There. You won't be going anywhere nor giving me trouble, now will you?"

144

She held up her hands. "It doesn't appear that I will be able to."

"Exactly. Let's go. Oh, but first..." He took the bandana from around his neck and gagged her with it. She thought she would lose her supper, but managed to keep it down.

He helped her into the saddle and climbed on behind her, then he rode close to the wagon train, though still in the dark until he was near her and Lydia's wagon. Taking a piece of paper from his pocket, he dismounted, tied the horse to a small tree, and ran to the wagon. He used a small knife to attach the note to the back gate of the wagon. Then he turned and ran back to where he left her in the dark, tied to the saddle so she couldn't run away.

She saw Lydia turn just as O'Toole started to run back. Hopefully, Lydia recognized him and would tell Mr. Gunn what had happened.

CHAPTER 11

By the time Joe doubled back and reached the wagon train night had settled and most were eating supper or had just finished. He rode directly to Lydia and Hannah's wagon.

He found Lydia in hysterics and Chester Gunn trying to calm her.

Joe slid from the saddle and ran to them.

"Where is Hannah?" He took Lydia by the shoulders and gave her a shake so she would stop crying and answer him. "Lydia! Where is Hannah?"

She handed him a piece of paper with a hole in the top.

He read the note.

"God damn it. Forgive me for my language. I was afraid of this. When did you get this message?"

When Lydia just continued to cry, Joe shook her again.

"Pull yourself together, Lydia. I need as much information as I can get."

She nodded, took a deep breath and wrapped her arms around her middle. "I'm sorry, Joe. What do you need from me?"

"How long ago did you get this?"

"About twenty minutes. Hannah went down to the river like she does every night, to get water for the dishes and to wash herself. She took one of the rifles so I didn't think anything about it. She'd been gone about ten minutes when I saw Mr. O'Toole running from our wagon. Stuck to the back gate of the wagon with a knife was this note."

Joe read the missive again.

I've got Hannah. I'll kill her if Joe doesn't give up looking for me. As he knows, I have no qualms about killing a woman. I'm already going to hang if they catch me. One more death isn't changing that. So why should I care about Hannah one way or the other.

"Will you stop following him?" asked Chester.

"I can't. If I do, I'll never get Hannah back."

Chester nodded. "That's what I figure, too. O'Toole is a fool."

Joe smiled. "Lucky for us, my Hannah is not a fool. O'Toole will have his hands full trying to get her cooperation."

O'Toole had her in the saddle and he rode behind her with his arm around her waist. Glad Joe taught her to ride, she leaned forward until she wasn't touching O'Toole. Her back was ramrod straight, and she didn't know how long she could keep the uncomfortable position.

After they'd gone a couple of miles and could no longer see the light from the wagon train, O'Toole slowed his horse.

"No sense riding him too hard. We're close to where I want to be."

Since she was still gagged, she didn't answer.

O'Toole took the bandana from her mouth.

"That was disgusting. The least you could have done was use a clean bandana."

"No need for one now. You can holler your fool head off, and no one, but *no one,* will hear you."

"No point in wasting my voice then is there? You're an evil man."

"That's what they said when I killed my wife and set the house on fire to get rid of her body. Unlucky for me, the fire didn't take very well and was quickly put out by the fire department. They found her with the single gunshot to the head and knew that I was the one who had done it."

He rode into a small draw and slid from the horse before pulling her down.

"Why would you kill your wife?"

"I was tired of her and there was a little blonde

dancer down at the saloon I had my eye on. Now, I know you can cook, so fix me supper."

"Where is your food? I can't cook with nothing to prepare." She held up her hands. "Or with my hands tied."

He turned and removed the ropes on her wrists. "There's flour and such in the saddlebags and some canned beans. No time to cook the dry ones."

While preparing the meal, she thought of Lydia, probably crying her eyes out instead of cooking. She was so tenderhearted, but she didn't know Joe.

Hannah wasn't afraid. She knew Joe would come for her. Believing in her husband, knowing that even if he didn't love her, she still belonged to him. He would come for her, she didn't doubt it. She'd just have to warn him about O'Toole.

When the biscuits were made and the beans heated, she called Mr. O'Toole back from where he was caring for his horse. *At least the man is good to his horse.*

"Your supper is ready."

"Good."

He picked up the rope from where she'd dropped it and retied her hands, he filled a tin plate with the beans and took two of the six biscuits she'd made.

He never offered her any of the food, though she didn't care. She wasn't hungry. She just wanted to go home. Home to Joe and Lydia and all her crazy pets.

"You know when Joe gets here, he'll kill you for what you did to me."

"He won't have a chance. He's off chasing after those two other men. He don't care about me and since you was forced on him, he'll be happy to get rid of you."

"You're wrong. You'll get yours in the end. All evil men do. Joe will make you pay for this... Lancaster."

"So he told you who I am. Makes no difference, so shut up before I put the gag back."

"Where do I sleep?"

"Wherever you want. If it were me, I'd sleep close to the fire."

"Where's my blanket?"

"You ain't got no blanket." He jutted his chin toward the fire and then cackled. "Another reason to set yourself close to the fire."

Even though it was summer and the day had been very warm, when the sun went down, so did the temperature. Hannah sat against a log and brought the back of her skirt up around her shoulders to help stop her shivering. She was still covered in back with her bloomers and petticoat besides she was against a log. Who was she showing anything to?

Her head lolled to one side and she woke with a start, just as a hand covered her mouth.

"Shhh, baby. It's just me." Joe whispered in her ear before he kissed the top of her head and removed his hand.

"Joe," she whispered then stood as quietly as she could. She held out her hands.

Joe removed the rope from her wrists and then drew his Colt revolver from his holster and pointed at O'Toole...Dick Lancaster.

As soon as Hannah was safely behind him, he yelled at Lancaster.

"Wake up you piece of crap."

Lancaster reached for his gun, but Joe shot the dirt next to him.

"You reach for that again, and you're a dead man. I should shoot you anyway for kidnapping my wife."

Lancaster sat up and raised his hands. "I didn't mean no harm. I just wanted to go far away."

"That's not happening today. And what made you think kidnapping Hannah would make me let you get away? What kind of thinking is that?"

"Well, I figured since you were forced to marry, that if she disappeared you'd be happy...free...and let me go."

"You figured wrong. I don't let anyone take what is mine. Hannah is mine. My wife and I'll never let her go."

Hannah felt tears spring into her eyes at Joe's words. He really wanted her. Love would come, she was sure of it. She swiped at her eyes while his attention was on Lancaster.

"He's lying, Joe. He intended to shoot you in the back when you came for me."

"Now, that I believe." He jutted his chin at Lancaster. "Drop your gun and kick it over to me."

Lancaster did as Joe said.

Joe's gun never wavered.

"Hannah, go pick up the weapon."

She came out and got the pistol, holding it pointing at the ground. Lancaster lunged forward and grabbing for the gun from her while keeping her between him and Joe.

As soon as he touched Hannah, Joe fired, hitting him in the shoulder and leg.

Lancaster collapsed on the ground.

Joe walked over to him. "You're one lucky man. I should have shot you dead."

The man rolled on the ground, holding his leg. "You got to get me to a doctor. You can't leave me like this."

"You're right I can't leave you. You're worth two-hundred-fifty dollars to me."

He looked at Hannah and smiled.

"To us."

She smiled back and handed him the gun, inordinately pleased he'd included her.

He put it in his waistband then he holstered his weapon.

"I guess we better get him on his horse. You hold the horse's reins and I'll get him into the saddle."

She picked up the reins and held them close to the bit.

Joe helped Lancaster into the saddle and had him hang on to the saddle horn.

"I hope you ride better than you shoot."

Lancaster sat slumped in the saddle, still pressing the wound on his leg. "Just get me to the doctor before I bleed to death."

Joe walked to Hannah, held her by the chin and looked at her intently.

"He hit you. You have a black eye. I'll kill him."

She reached for his shoulder as he turned around. "No, Joe. He'll hang for what he did. I don't want you to hang with him. I know the poster says dead or alive, but don't lower yourself. I'm fine. This is a badge of courage. Proof I fought back. Proof he's a coward."

He took her in his arms and kissed her thoroughly.

"I missed you."

"I missed you, too," she said and meant it. She was glad he'd be with her again tonight.

He lifted her into the saddle then mounted behind her. He held her with one arm around her waist and the other hand held the reins of his horse and Lancaster's mount.

"We'll be staying at the fort tonight. I figure, as long as we have to go there and drop him off, we might as well stay and take advantage of their hospitality."

She nodded. "Sounds good. Sleeping in a soft bed is most welcome."

Joe leaned forward and whispered. "Who said anything about sleeping?"

Hannah's eyes widened. She knew exactly what he was referring to and she wouldn't stop him or slow him down this time. She wanted to consummate this marriage as much or more than he did.

She chuckled. "You're a scandalous man, Joe Stanton."

"Only with my wife, Hannah Stanton."

Hannah liked that he called her his wife. She liked that he seemed to be content with her. Both those things boded well for having a happy marriage. The only thing missing was love for each other, but she was sure that would come. It had to.

She couldn't imagine being the only one in love. Joe would come around and maybe he already did love her but didn't know it. He treated her like he loved her. He was more than kind, teased her mercilessly and hinted at all sorts of naughty things, like making love all night...that wasn't possible...was it?

By the time they reached Fort Laramie, the sun was almost straight up, noon. She was starving and wanted to eat before they did anything else.

Joe left Hannah on the horse while he escorted Dick Lancaster into the office of Colonel Roger Travers.

The post doctor examined the prisoner, declaring his wounds were not life-threatening and he would be laid up for a few weeks.

Colonel Travers stood at the end of the hospital bed while the doctor worked on Lancaster. "You'll be in the stockade until you're healed enough for the journey back to Independence, where you'll stand trial for murdering your wife, kidnapping Mrs. Hannah Stanton and attempted murder of Joe Stanton. More than likely you'll face the hangman's rope."

Lancaster's eyes were wild, shooting back and forth. He yelled at the top of his lungs. "I'll be out of here and free in no time. They can't prove I did anything. You'll see."

"You keep believing that," said Joe.

"We'll see he gets to his cell and gets his wounds treated. How did he come to be wounded?"

"He put his hands on Hannah."

Joe didn't need to say anything else. Roger Travers was his friend and knew exactly what had happened from those six words.

"I'm taking Hannah to our room after she sees her sister. I'm glad the wagon train didn't leave yet."

"I'll make sure it's ready for you. Chester Gunn and I had a little talk and both agreed they would go ahead and stay for the full three days."

"Thanks, Rog. I appreciate it."

"I owe you many times over for all the times

you saved my hide. The least I can do is give you and your new wife a room for the night."

The men shook hands and Joe went back out to where Hannah stood on the colonel's porch in the shade. She leaned against the side of the building and pushed away when Joe came out of the office.

"Get too hot on the horse?"

"Yes and too noticeable."

"That was bad judgment on my part. I didn't think dropping off Lancaster would take as long as it did. I'm sorry."

"No harm done. I didn't melt."

He chuckled. "No, thank goodness, you didn't melt. Let's go see Lydia and let her know you are safe and sound."

"I bet she'll have something to eat, too."

He put his arm around her shoulders. "Hungry? Why didn't you say so? I have hardtack and jerky in my saddle bags."

She looked away. "That's why I didn't say anything. I didn't want to have to refuse you."

Joe laughed. "I don't suppose those offerings are very appetizing."

She shook her head. "Only if I was really and truly starving. And even then, I'd think twice." *Or three times or more. I definitely would have to be so hungry my stomach would think my throat had been cut.*

They rode up to their wagon.

Joe dismounted and then held up his arms to Hannah.

She leaned down and put her hands on his shoulders while he lifted her to the ground.

As soon as her feet touched the dirt, she took off toward Lydia.

"Lydie!" She called using her childhood name for her sister. "Lydie!"

Lydia ran toward her from where she sat by the fire. Sampson followed.

They fell into each other's arms.

"I knew Joe would find you. Thank God. Oh, thank God."

She pulled back from Hannah, held her at arm's length and looked her up and down.

"Are you all right? You have a black eye. He hit you?"

"Don't worry about it. I'm fine, Lydie. Fine. Except—"

"Except what?"

"I'm starving. Do you have any food for two hungry people?"

Lydia laughed. "I always have food. Come, eat." She looked up at Joe. "Come on brother-in-law of mine. Eat."

She held open an arm to Joe.

He came and put his arm around Lydia's waist so she was in the middle and Hannah was on the other side.

They walked like that to the wagon where Lydia let them go.

"Sit. Sit. I'll have lunch served in no time."

They sat on a large boulder. She brought them each a plate of rabbit stew and fresh biscuits with butter.

Hannah didn't think she'd tasted anything as great as Lydia's stew. She ate quickly and would have eaten a second plate but knew she needed to let the first one settle, or she'd make herself sick.

"What about the other two men?" asked Lydia. "Are you going after them?"

"I haven't decided yet."

Hannah touched his arm. "Of course, you will. You can't let them get away with their crimes."

"I'd rather let them go than have you in danger again."

"I won't have such a cavalier attitude. This taught me a lesson. As much as I think I can take care of myself, there are times, I can't. From now on I'll be more cautious. I'll get water when it's light out or not at all. We have good water in the barrels on the wagon. I want to keep that replenished for the desert crossing coming up, but hopefully, we'll be warned when we reach the last water before we cross the mountains."

"You will. Everyone will want to fill up. Luckily it's a very good spring. Everyone should get all the water they need, but there is nothing wrong with saving your water. As a matter of fact, it's a good idea."

Hannah smiled wide.

"But only if you can get the water from the river in the daylight," said Joe.

She nodded. "Agreed. Or I'll get together with some others and we can go in a group. That will be safer."

"I'll be here to go with you. Those two men are headed west. I can stay with the wagon train as we travel west and see if they've shown up anywhere. If not, then I'll hunt them after we get you settled in Oregon City."

"You're staying?" Heat radiated through her chest and she felt light. She smiled wide. "I'm so glad. We need to get to know each other and learning about the other is hard to do if you're not here."

He frowned. "Be aware that if I haven't caught them by the time we reach Oregon City, I'll have to leave and go after them. You're right, I can't let them get away with their crimes."

"I understand. How long is the rest of the journey?"

"We're about a third of the way, so it'll be about four more months. Why?"

Hannah looked and saw Lydia at the wagon feeding Simba. She said softly, "I wonder if I can get pregnant by then."

Joe furrowed his eyebrows. "Why is that important? When you get with child, I mean?"

"Because then, when you go away, I still have part of you and I have someone who'll love me unconditionally."

Joe didn't say anything, but Hannah saw the change in his expression and his demeanor.

"Hannah, I'm sorry—"

She stiffened and placed two fingers against his lips.

"You have no need to be sorry. Ours wasn't a love match, I know that. Someday, we might find that we love each other and we may not, but at least we'll always be friends. Special friends."

Joe nodded and kissed her fingers. "Always friends."

If he noticed the sadness in her eyes, he didn't mention it, and neither did she.

CHAPTER 12

"That stew was a fine meal, Lydia. My compliments to the chef," said Joe when Lydia returned to the campfire.

She waved away his words. "Oh, Joe. You are always saying such nice things."

Hannah agreed with her sister. Joe had a silver tongue.

"I only state the facts. But if you will excuse us, we've been up all night and need a few hours of shut-eye."

She nodded. "I thought you might. I've packed a bag for Hannah."

Lydia went to the wagon and grabbed a carpet bag from inside the rear of the conveyance.

"That is so nice of you. What did you put in it?" asked Hannah.

"Just a nightgown and a complete change of clothes for tomorrow."

Hannah took the bag from Lydia and held it in front of her with both hands. "Perfect."

"Shall we go?" asked Joe, taking the luggage from Hannah.

"Yes. I'm ready."

Joe took her hand in his and led her to his horse. He tied the suitcase to the back of the saddle and then helped Hannah into the saddle. When she was seated he mounted behind her and took the reins.

"Bye, Lydia. See you at supper," called Hannah.

"Not if I can help it," whispered Joe. "I intend to make you mine. Are you ready for that?"

Hannah swallowed hard and took a deep breath. "I'm ready. I want to be your wife in all ways, not just in name only."

"That's my girl."

He touched his boots to the horse's sides and the stallion began to trot. Another touch of his heels and the gait became a canter, much easier for the riders.

When they entered the fort they rode directly to the stable. The horse must be taken care of before they could enjoy each other.

Joe handed Hannah her bag.

She set it on the ground. "Can I help?"

"If you'd get a bag of oats for him I'd appreciate it. He deserves every morsel for finding you."

"I'm certainly glad you did. I was afraid I might suffer more abuse at his hands."

Joe stared at her. "I'd still like to kill him for that bruise he gave you."

She reached up and tenderly touched her cheek. The bruise was under her eye not right on top of it.

"I'd rather you didn't. I'm ready for you to make love to me. Are you ready?"

He grinned.

From the stable, she and Joe walked back to Old Bedlam and the room on the corner of the first floor.

He carried the suitcase, and when they arrived at the room, he opened the door but didn't let Hannah enter. Instead, he scooped her into his arms.

Hannah gasped and wrapped her arms around his neck.

"If you keep carrying me around, you'll throw out your back. I'm too heavy."

Joe grinned. "You're not too heavy for me. You're just right."

She smiled and relaxed in his arms. Joe was strong. He carried her and the suitcase into the room, shutting the door behind them with a well-placed kick.

He dropped the carpet bag and then let Hannah slide down his body to the floor.

She felt every hard inch of him. When she was

safely down, Joe took her face between his palms, lowered his head and took her lips with his.

Hannah felt his kiss clear to her toes.

He pressed his tongue against her lips silently pleading for entrance, while his arms circled her waist and pressed her against him.

She granted it, almost as anxious to taste him as he seemed to be her.

Finally, he pulled back but kept his arms around her.

"I want you naked. I'll do my best not to hurt you but this first time, there will be some pain, but never again."

"I'm not afraid. Not with you."

"Good. I'm glad. I don't want to talk at all. Just feel."

Hannah nodded.

Joe unfastened the top button on her dress. Followed by another and another until it was open below her waist and he could slide the garment off her arms. As he did, he kissed the column of her neck and then the top of her breasts, through her chemise.

Hannah felt like she was wearing a corset. She found it hard to draw a deep breath, instead, almost panted. Her body ached, and the center of her womanhood seemed liquid, moving, flowing, pulsing. She held his head to her body wanting more of his kisses and more of all the sensations he gave her.

Joe chuckled and grasped her hands by the wrists and held them away from his head.

"You are so passionate. Let's get the rest of these clothes off of you."

She liked that he thought her passionate, if she only knew exactly what that meant.

He untied her chemise and let it open.

She pulled it over her head.

He tugged the bow in the string on her bloomers and then loosened it so the clothing fell down her legs to pool around her ankles.

"God, you're beautiful."

She stood stiff, her arms to her sides.

"Darlin' relax."

"How can I relax when I'm the only one naked?"

"That is something that can be remedied right now."

Quicker than lightning, Joe was out of his clothes and stood before her nude, proud and completely ready for her.

Joe scooped her into his arms and took her to the bed, laying her in the middle and then he lay next to her, propped on one elbow.

Hannah stayed stiff as a board and tried very hard not to touch Joe. He had no such qualms.

I'm scared. Making love is unlike anything I can relate to. What if I don't make love right?

Joe ran a hand down her arm, then over and down the center of her body, between her breasts.

Hannah shivered. She couldn't help her reaction to his fingers lightly teasing her skin as they moved down her body. He circled her breasts and then tweaked her nipples before moving on down to rest on her mound.

"Joe, don't stop. Don't tell me this is all there is, please."

"No, sweetheart, we are just getting started."

Joe made love to her with his mouth. He prepared her as best he could for his entry into her body, for which she was very grateful.

After they made love, they lay in bed, holding each other and listening to their heartbeats.

Hanna let her fingers play in the sparse hair on Joe's chest. "Love making is amazing."

"Yeah. And we'll get better and better at making love, as time goes by."

"Do you think we made a baby?"

"I don't know, but I doubt it. I think it takes most people months before the wife gets with child."

"Well, I hope we're not like most people. I hope I get pregnant right away."

"I'm voting for lots of practice."

"You're funny and quite outrageous."

"I'm serious. I want to make love to you often and in many ways. I want to unlock your passion."

"I'm only this way with you, so you can take your time to…unlock…me." She giggled.

Joe laughed and pulled her tighter.

"If you weren't sore, we'd go for round two, but making love again will have to wait. For now, we should take a nap. Neither of us got any sleep last night and if we are to be decent company at supper, we need the rest."

Hannah stifled one yawn but the second one came out full force.

"See?"

"I am tired and yet I feel amazing."

He squeezed her close. "Close your eyes and dream of me."

"That's easy. I always do."

She cuddled into his side, her head resting on his arm and her arm over his chest. He was so warm.

He pulled the blankets over them.

"Hannah. Wake up, sweetheart."

"Hmmm." She scrunched deeper into her pillow.

"Come on, now. Wake up."

She shook her head and wished the sounds would go away.

Joe shook her shoulder. "Hannah!"

She jerked upright. "What? What?"

"Wake up. We're late. Come on. Get dressed."

Hannah jumped out of bed, unmindful of her state of nakedness. She grabbed her undergarments and put them on then took her clean dress from the carpet bag and pulled it over her head. When she'd finished dressing she looked at herself in the mirror and groaned.

"My hair. I hope Lydia packed my brush and comb."

She shouldn't have worried. In the bottom of the bag was her brush set. Taking the brush, she gently pulled it through her tangled tresses until no more tangles existed and she could gather it at the back of her head in a bun.

"I still like your hair down better."

"I know, but wearing my hair down in public would be totally improper, especially since I'm married now."

Joe sat on the bed, pulled on his boots and grumbled. "Too many rules about what is proper and what isn't."

Hannah smiled at his grumpiness. Good to know he wasn't so easy going all the time.

September 1, 1852

The wagon train was nearly to South Pass, almost two-thirds of the way to Oregon City.

Joe pointed at the low saddle of prairie land that was almost flat. "This is the safest and easiest place to cross the Rocky Mountains. The Sweetwater River flows on the east side of the pass. We'll camp there for the night, restock our water supplies and rest the animals for the journey over the pass."

Joe and Hannah were returning from a short morning ride. Hannah wanted to see more of the country and, if they had the chance, to make love. She was discovering it was hard to have time alone even at night, in the cramped space under the wagon or when they shared the tent with Lydia and her menagerie.

As they approached the wagon train, Hannah saw smoke roiling high up in the air.

She pointed toward the wagons. "Joe, the smoke. Do you think a wagon is on fire?"

"I don't know, but I wouldn't bet against it."

"Hurry. I need to make sure Lydia is all right."

They rode hard to get to the train. Chaos reigned. People were running everywhere. The wagon on fire *was* the Granger wagon and Lydia was nowhere to be seen. "God, where is she?"

Chester Gunn directed people away from the fire.

Dear God. Hannah prayed. *Please let her be safe.*

Suddenly, from the river side of the wagons walked Lydia, holding the kitten and the cub, with Sampson following at her heels.

"Stop," demanded Hannah. "There she is."

Joe slid from the horse at the same time as Hannah.

As soon as her feet hit the ground Hannah raced toward Lydia.

"Are you all right? What happened?"

Lydia blinked slowly and looked around her

frowning. Her hair was askew, sticking up all over. Soot covered her face and clothes. "I don't know really. They tell me it was a flaming arrow and they're looking for an Indian now, but I don't believe it. The only Indians we've come across have been peaceful."

"Were you in the wagon when the fire started?" asked Joe.

"No. I went in after the babies. I couldn't let them die in there." She nuzzled Trinity and Simba. The tiny cub didn't move very much, unlike Trinity who was doing his best to get out of Lydia's hold.

Hannah knew there was nothing she could do about the fire, but pray it wasn't as bad as it looked. But Simba she could help. "Let me see Simba."

Lydia handed her the baby cougar.

"We need to get the smoke off of him. The more he breathes in the smoke, the worse off he'll be."

"Let's go to the river. You can bathe him and Lydia can wash up, too," said Joe.

Hannah noticed he kept his hand over his gun as he scanned the crowd.

Suddenly he stopped and narrowed his eyes.

She looked in the direction he was looking and saw Mr. Smith and Mr. Jones milling with the people on the bucket brigade. Hannah knew to her very soul, they were the ones who set the fire. What were they trying to achieve? Were they after Joe?

Joe put his arm around her shoulders and

leaned down to whisper. "I'll get around behind them. I don't want anyone else to be hurt. I'm the one they're looking for."

Her gut clenched. "What if you're not? I admit the situation does look that way since they burned our wagon but we have no proof—"

"I have all the proof I need. They circled back after having escaped. O'Toole kidnapped you. He could have been in cahoots with these two, and they're looking for you or him. I'm not letting that happen. They are wanted by the law. I will take them down."

"Be careful. I'm not ready to be a widow."

Joe grinned. "I'm not ready to make you one."

He gave her a quick kiss and blended in with the crowd, working ever closer to the two men.

The bucket brigade poured water on the wagon. Thank goodness they were next to the river. When the wagon fire was out, she saw the damage wasn't as extensive as they feared it would be. They'd lost the wagon cover, maybe a blanket or two and a nearly empty bag of flour. They were lucky. Mr. Gunn had been there quickly, cut the ropes holding on the cover and pulled it away from the wagon. He'd saved them and saved their journey. If he hadn't, they would have had to go back to Fort Laramie and stay until they earned enough money to resume the trip.

Hannah heard gunfire and started running toward the place she'd seen Smith and Jones. When she arrived, two bodies lay on the ground. One was Mr. Jones.

The other was Joe.

Her stomach dropped to her knees and her heart raced. "Joe!"

CHAPTER 13

He was breathing but badly wounded. He had a wound in his shoulder just above his heart. An inch or so lower and he'd be dead.

She ripped a strip off her petticoat and used it to staunch the flow of blood from the shoulder wound.

He'd been shot in his thigh too, but the injury wasn't bleeding badly, so she ignored it for now.

Chester Gunn came up to her.

"Jones is dead. There's a blood trail leading off into the weeds but it ends near the river. We found Jones' horse and signs of another one. Smith's wounded, Hannah. He'll have to seek medical attention somewhere. We'll find him."

"I don't care about him. I care about Joe." *What if he dies? Dear God, please don't let him die. I just found him, don't take him from me.*

Gunn put a hand on her shoulder. "I'll take care of Joe. It won't be the first time I've patched him up."

He looked up and signaled to a couple of men. They came over and picked up Joe.

Chester watched them for a minute and then turned his gaze back on Hannah. "They're taking him to my wagon. You're more than welcome to stay there and tend to him after I remove the bullets."

She pulled her shoulders back and her back ramrod straight. "Of course, I will. Thank you, Mr. Gunn."

"I figure since you're now the wife of my good friend, you should call me Chester."

"Very well, Chester, I will be staying with Joe. What about Lydia?"

"She can come, too. If we can we'll use your tent to make a new cover for the wagon. Then she'll be able to stay there with her pets."

Hannah nodded. "Thank you. I know she'll appreciate it."

Chester had the men put Joe in his wagon.

"That's right men, right there in the middle on those blankets. Then please take the tarp from the back of the chuck wagon and wrap Jones in it. Joe has a bounty coming for that man. We'll turn him in at Fort Bridger, just the other side of South Pass." He turned back to Hannah. "They should have a doctor at Fort Bridger. We may have to leave Joe there."

She shook her head. "He wouldn't want to stay. I'll tend to him for the rest of the journey. He'll be up and around long before we reach Oregon City. He'll want to go after Mr. Smith. He deserves the opportunity to avenge himself and finish his job."

Chester smiled. "I guess you do know him. Vengence is exactly what he'll want and he wouldn't be forgiving me for leaving him behind."

"Good. Now get those bullets out of him while he's unconscious. I'll stitch him up after. Hopefully, he'll remain out for the duration of the treatment."

Hannah retrieved her sewing kit from her damaged wagon. When she returned, Chester had removed the bullets and was pouring whiskey in the wounds.

"You can sew him up now. I've done the best I can do for him."

She made quick work of stitching her husband's injuries closed. Luckily Joe didn't regain consciousness.

Lydia came to the back of the wagon, the little cub in her arms. Only he wasn't so little anymore. He grew like a weed, though he was still a baby and Trinity ruled the roost.

"You should come get something to eat."

"I need—"

Lydia held up a hand. "You need to take care of yourself, so you can take care of Joe. I don't want to be the only one that's healthy enough to treat you both."

She placed her wrist on his forehead to check for fever. He was cool and dry. "All right. Joe should be fine without me for a little while."

"Yes, he should. I'll bring the food over here so you can hear him should he awake. Fair enough?"

Hannah nodded. "Fair enough. You're a good sister, Lydie."

Lydia smiled. "I have to take care of my big sister."

"I'm your only sister."

Lydia chuckled. "Well, there is that."

For the first time in two days, Hannah relaxed a bit. Joe was still unconscious and that worried her, but Lydia was right. She had to take care of herself if she was to help Joe.

She'd just finished her dinner when she heard moans coming from the wagon. Hannah set her plate on the ground and raced to the wagon, climbing into the back by way of stairs that folded down. They made it much easier than getting in and out of her wagon which didn't have stairs.

"Joe." She brushed his dark hair back from his forehead and laid her cheek on it. She gasped. His skin was way too warm. "Can you hear me?"

"Hannah. Hannah!" He struggled to sit up. "Got to save her."

"I'm fine, Joe. It's me, Hannah."

He opened his eyes wide, reached up and touched her face. "So beautiful. How did I ever get so lucky?"

Then he closed his eyes and, thrashing back and forth, fought demons only he could see.

She stroked his arms and talked to him. When he heard her voice he would settle for a moment, but then before too long, he'd be fighting again. For a day and a half, Hannah wiped his body with washcloths rinsed in cold water from the river. Finally, his fever broke and he recognized her and Chester and remembered the gunfight.

"I think I hit both Smith and Jones. Were they wounded?"

"You killed Jones," said Chester, who sat just inside the back of the wagon. "We have his body on the way to the sheriff in South Pass City now. We pulled up outside town last night."

Joe looked over at Hannah. "Water. Please."

"Of course. I'll get you some fresh. Be right back." She climbed out the back of the wagon, past Chester.

Joe watched Hannah go and then whispered to Chester. "Tell me about Smith and hurry, I don't want Hannah to hear."

Chester shook his head. "She already knows it all. Wouldn't let us take you to the doctor. I was going to leave you there to recuperate, but Hannah wouldn't hear of it. She insisted you had the right to go after the man who shot you."

"She did?"

Hannah appeared at the back of the wagon. "Yes. She did."

Joe grinned. "I picked a good one, don't you think, Chester?"

"I know so. She's one in a million."

"You two will make me blush. But don't think I'm so great yet, because I insist on accompanying Joe when he goes after Smith."

Joe propped himself on his elbows. "Gawd, don't make me move like that. Where was I wounded?

"In the shoulder and the leg."

"Hannah, you will not be coming with me. Absolutely not."

"You don't have any choice. If you don't let me go with you, I'll follow you on my own."

"It's too dangerous." He waved his hand over his body. "Look at me. This could be you lying here, wounded."

"That is just the point, seeing you wounded scared the hell out of me. I won't lose you. I won't let you leave me a widow without doing my level best to prevent it."

Joe's mouth formed a thin line. "When I'm better, you and I will talk again."

"I agree. This conversation is not good to be having while you're trying to heal and get rest."

He closed his eyes and grumbled.

Hannah had to lean closer to hear what he was saying.

"Damn fool woman."

She smiled. He was feeling better. Now she just had to convince him to let her go with him.

It had been nearly a month since the shootout with Smith and Jones. The sheriff in South Pass City paid the money for Jones' bounty, five hundred dollars, dead or alive, and his deputies buried his body.

Joe took off the sling that Hannah and Chester insisted he wear. He looked at his hand as he made fist after fist. Loosening his fingers and reminding them who was boss.

Next, he drew his weapon. Slow, very slow and his muscles twinged. He would have to find another way to subdue his bounties, until his expertise returned.

Joe cussed and slammed his fisted left hand into his right. He and Hannah attended the burial. Joe had hoped Jones' friend, Mr. Smith, would show up for it, but no such luck. Or, if he had, Joe never saw him.

The wagon train pushed on. They had to cross the Wind River Range and the Blue Mountains before winter weather made the crossing more difficult and dangerous.

South Pass City was a mining community, and men outnumbered women about ninety-nine to one.

The miners arranged a dance, and the brides all attended. Joe even took Hannah, much to her surprise and delight.

She donned her pink silk dress. When she stepped out of the wagon she heard a whistle.

Turning toward the fire, she saw Joe, standing next to Lydia, holding a cup of coffee.

She smiled and walked to them.

Joe looked from her to Lydia and back again. "You look beautiful, ladies. Shall we go?"

She and Lydia each took one of Joe's arms and they walked to the dance.

Hannah danced and danced, with Joe and Chester, and with the miners. A few of the brides decided to stay and marry the miner they'd met. They said marrying the miner they'd come to like was better than marrying some unknown man.

She couldn't fault them their logic. After all, she'd not wanted to marry a strange man. As it was, she was lucky because she fell in love with Joe. Now, if he could just love her back.

Before the dance was over, as she and Joe walked back to the wagon, Hannah decided to tell him her news.

Chester said he would escort Lydia home after the dance was over.

"I've got something I need to tell you."

"Let me guess. Lydia's decided to stay and marry one of these miners."

She frowned. "No, of course, not. That wouldn't be honorable."

Joe laughed.

He was in a very good mood which boded well.

"We're having a baby." Hannah blurted the information out and didn't stop walking.

Joe stopped in his tracks.

"Baby? Did you say, baby?"

She heard him before she felt his hand on her shoulder stopping her.

He turned her to face him. "Are you sure?"

She nodded. "I'm sure. I think it happened the first time we were together. Remember how I wished for it?"

"I remember."

Then he swung her into his arms and spun in a circle.

"We're having a baby."

She laughed and held on. He set her down and held her hand for the walk back to the wagon.

"Joe, you love this baby, right?"

"Of course. It's a part of each of us."

"Do you love me?" she whispered the words.

He was quiet for far too long, so she knew he'd heard her.

"I'm sorry. I shouldn't have asked the question. I thought maybe you could love me by now, too."

She looked straight ahead and clasped her hands in front of her.

"If I could love a woman it would be you. But I can't. I don't know how anymore. That feeling evades me."

Fighting tears, she talked past the lump in her throat. "I understood why you didn't want an annulment, but why can't you feel love for me? I'm very sorry for what Sandra did to you. But being abandoned can't happen again. Don't you see? You and I are already married. We're starting a family in about seven months or so."

He scrubbed his hands over his face. "You think I don't know all that? You think I don't want to love you? Dammit, I don't know how to. Just leave it be."

They walked in silence until they reached the wagon.

Joe helped her up but didn't follow.

"I'm going for a walk. I need to clear my head."

Sad and feeling abandoned, she nonetheless cupped his face with a hand. "As you wish. I'll be here. I won't go anywhere, Joe. I'll always be here for you, wherever here may be."

He closed his eyes and leaned ever so slightly into her palm. Then he straightened.

His reaction as though he remembered he wasn't supposed to love her. *You're a contradiction, Joe Stanton. One I will figure out. I will always love you, whether you love me or not. I just don't know if I'm*

*lying when I say I'll always be here. I don't know if I can
stay in a marriage with no love.*

*Then again, how can I not? I don't want to raise a
child alone, especially a child who is loved by his father. I
can't be so cruel.*

Joe came to bed late. They stayed in the tent
they'd bought in South Pass City. The old tent
served as a cover for the wagon where Lydia slept.

This arrangement allowed them a modicum of
privacy, for which Hannah was grateful. She and
Joe could make love on occasion and, like tonight,
they could talk without being overheard.

"Are you feeling better after your walk?"

"Yes, but I owe you an apology."

"No, you don't. I shouldn't have brought up the
subject."

He lay down beside her and lifted an arm for
her to cuddle.

She scooted next to him and placed an arm over
his chest, and then settled her head on his shoulder.

They kept to their promise not to go to bed
angry, even when doing so was difficult, as it was
now.

"I care for you, Hannah. More than I ever
expected to, more than I have anyone else in a long,
long time."

Her heartbeat quickened. "I'm glad. I care for
you, too."

"Is that enough for you?"

"It has to be. I won't give up on this marriage. We're having a baby, Joe. A baby that deserves to have two parents. Don't you think so, too?"

"I do. But—"

"No buts. We are staying married. We decided that before we ever consummated this union. I see no reason to change our minds now."

He squeezed her shoulders. "You're amazing, Hannah. Do you know that?"

"Of course. You wouldn't have married me, no matter the reason, if you hadn't wanted to and that in itself proves I'm amazing." She giggled, turned and kissed his chest.

He laughed and pulled her on top of him, wrapping her in his arms, and then brought her head down for a kiss.

The conversation about love was forgotten for now as they made love as quietly as possible in the tent in the middle of the wagon train's circle.

Tomorrow they would cross the Wind River Range. She'd been told the trip was dangerous and wasn't looking forward to it.

Some of the women told stories they'd heard of wagons being lost in some of the steep gorges they would have to cross.

She shuddered and cuddled closer, hoping they were just stories. But what if they weren't?

CHAPTER 14

The sound of the morning bugle came earlier than usual or so it seemed to Hannah. As quickly as possible, she threw back the blankets and scurried out of bed and into her day clothes. Then she went out of the tent and found Lydia already up and feeding her brood.

She'd added an owlet to her menagerie. The little bird had been sitting by the water's edge, just sitting there lost. Lydia told Hannah that when she approached he started hopping up and down and beating his wings. Poor little thing didn't know how to fly yet, and Lydia hadn't seen any other birds. She'd actually climbed the tree to the nest and found it empty.

So she picked up the tiny owl and added it to her other babies. She'd made a makeshift perch in the top of the wagon, so neither Trinity nor Simba could bother him. At each meal she fed him bits of raw meat. What she'd feed him when they ran out of meat, Hannah didn't know. Maybe, by that time, he'd figure out how to hunt for himself. She didn't know that, either. They'd never had an owl for a pet before.

As they approached the east side of the Wind River Range, she saw a trail winding its way up the mountain and not looking the least bit inviting.

From atop Maisy, Hannah pointed toward the path. "I don't like the looks of that road."

Joe rode next to her on Midnight, his big, black stallion, his expression grim. "We don't have any choice. We have to cross these mountains and the Blue Mountains before winter sets in. If we don't you'll learn about a whole different kind of treacherous. Now they're just frightening."

"Lydia and I will take turns in the wagon. I don't want either one of us to have the stress of driving it all the way."

"You won't." Joe clenched his jaw. "I'm driving the wagon. I want you two to walk behind it. I don't need you in the way if things go wrong up there."

Hannah shook her head. "No, I—"

"This is not up for discussion. I know the road, you two don't. I'm much more likely to get the wagon over the mountains safely than you are. There will be places where we will have to use a rope as a brake to keep the wagons from going over a cliff as they travel down the steep incline. I'm driving."

Hannah took a deep breath. His explanation scared her but she vowed she'd hide her fear. She would not give him something else to worry about. "You're right and I won't argue. We'll stay behind the wagon and out of your hair. I don't want you to worry about us. You'll have plenty on your mind as it is."

He leaned on the pommel with both arms crossed. "Thank you. I really hate that we always butt heads when I'm just working to keep you safe."

"I know. I'm sorry. I'm used to making my own decisions and only having to worry about Lydia. Now I have you." She touched her stomach. "And our baby to think of as well."

"We'll start up the mountain tomorrow. We need to try and get all fifty wagons to the top all in one day. The wagons can park at the top and stay safe until morning at the top. We definitely don't want them to be strung up the side of the mountain for the night if we can help it. The road down the other side is little more than an animal trail and goes beside some deep ravines."

Hannah put her hands on her fluttering stomach. "You're scaring me, Joe."

From his horse he extended his arm toward her.

She grabbed his hand and squeezed it.

"Good. I mean to scare you. I want both you and

Lydia to be alert and aware. Her animals will have to ride contained in the wagon. They could spook an ox or a horse without meaning to. We can't have that."

"I'll tell her."

He let her go and stepped back. "I have to talk to Chester. I'll be back in time for breakfast. Then we'll want to break camp fast. We have to get to the bottom of the pass over the Wind River Range, by the end of today. Moving all the wagons may mean traveling longer in a day than anyone is used to."

"Don't worry. We'll clean and pack as we go, so we'll be ready to leave shortly after breakfast."

"See you in about an hour."

"I'll be waiting on pins and needles."

Joe smiled and then left.

Hannah dismounted and went to find Lydia. She rounded the back of the wagon and found her with all her pets.

"Lydie."

The woman looked up.

"Yes."

Hannah stood with her legs apart and her arms crossed over her stomach. The gesture made her feel safer somehow. She had to keep her baby safe no matter what. "We'll get to the trail head today and cross the mountains tomorrow. Joe says the trip very dangerous and your animals must ride in the wagon. No questions. I told him they would."

"But they like—"

"Lydia! Didn't you hear me? The trip into and out of these mountains is too dangerous. If your animals spook a horse or ox and their wagon goes off the cliff, what will you say then?"

Lydia closed her eyes and hung her head for a moment. "I'm sorry. You're right. I was thinking about what was best for the animals and forgetting what was best for the people. I'm truly sorry. I don't want anyone hurt because of my animals."

"Good. Now I told Joe we'd cook and clean at the same time so that we're practically ready to go as soon as breakfast is over. He said Chester will want to get on the road as quickly as possible this morning. We have to reach the base of the mountains before we can stop tonight."

Lydia looked toward the mountains. "That's a long way."

"It is, so we want to be ready to leave as soon as Joe says "let's go"."

"All right, I'll fix breakfast while you do the other chores."

"When I'm done, I'll help you with breakfast. You cook and I'll wash the pans."

Hannah looked up from the sideboard of the wagon where she was washing the dishes. She dried her hands when she saw Joe walking toward her.

"What did Chester say?"

"I was right. We're leaving early. I supposed to tell all the wagons behind us and he'll get all the ones in front of us."

"Breakfast will be ready by the time you return."

He took Hannah in his arms and just held her for a minute. Then, he abruptly released her, turned and walked to the next wagon.

She knew the coming days weighed heavily on Joe. She was determined he wouldn't have to worry about her or Lydia. They would follow his instructions to the letter. She wouldn't fight with him on this.

Joe walked up to them just as Lydia was taking the Dutch oven full of biscuits off the fire.

"Perfect timing," she chirped to Joe.

He stopped and lifted a brow. "You seem awfully cheerful this morning, Lydia."

"Just ready to be on our way again. Isn't the Wind River Range more than two-thirds of the way to Oregon City?"

"It is. We'll have another month or so to go when we finish this crossing."

Lydia removed the Dutch oven full of biscuits from the fire. "I guess I'm getting a little nervous. I'll be meeting Mr. Mosley. What if after he meets me…and my pets…he doesn't want to marry me?"

Joe smiled. "There's no way in the world that he won't want to marry you, unusual pets and all. Anyone in their right mind would want to have you for a wife. But if he doesn't that won't be a problem. Your problem will be trying to decide who, and if, you want to marry. Trust me, you won't have any problems attracting a man to wed."

"That's what I keep telling her." Hannah waited to take the Dutch oven after Lydia took the biscuits out.

She placed all the biscuits on a tin plate and handed the pot to Hannah. "Thanks, Joe. That is reassuring."

"Anytime. Now, shall we eat and then get on the road? Chester wants me to take the lead since I've been over the trail before and he'll bring up the rear. If our wagon makes good time and get to the trail early, we're supposed to go ahead and start up the mountain. That way we can find any trouble spots and hopefully fix them before everyone else comes up."

"Well, your breakfast is ready." Hannah handed him a plate piled high with scrambled eggs, pancakes, bacon and two biscuits.

"This looks great. Thanks." He put a forkful of scrambled eggs into his mouth. "Mmm. Wonderful."

Hannah grinned. "You can thank Lydia. She did the cooking this morning."

"It's great as always. Thanks, sister-in-law."

Lydia chuckled. "You're welcome, brother-in-law."

It was time to leave and Hannah was anxious to get on the road.

Joe led the way on his horse and Hannah walked on the right of the oxen while Lydia drove the team from the left side, cracking the whip high above their heads to keep them moving. Maisy was tied behind the wagon with the two cows.

They arrived at the base of the Wind River Range at about three o'clock in the afternoon, having made very good time.

Joe rested the animals and let them graze while they prepared their own food.

"If we're eating tonight, it better be now," said Joe. "Camping on the trail is difficult and we don't want to go to much trouble except for doing the bedding. We won't get to eat again until we reach the top and then we can set up a real camp."

"That's fine. I'll start the meal. I don't know whether to call it lunch or supper," said Hannah. "Lydia will have to care for her animals and that can take a while. It's almost the bigger they get the more care they need."

Joe looked toward Lydia and shook his head. "She'll have problems because of those animals. You wait and see."

"That might be true. Maybe if she was certain they were going into loving homes she'd give them up, but who will take a full grown wolf or mountain lion into their home, regardless of how gentle they are?" She lifted a brow. "I know you wouldn't...even though they both adore you."

He frowned. "You're right about that. I don't want a wild animal, regardless of how supposedly tame it is, in my home."

"What about regular dogs and cats? How do you feel about pets?"

"Because of my job, it wouldn't be fair to the animal for me to be gone so long. I've never had one, so I don't know how to feel. It would bond with whoever tended it and then when I returned, the animal would be given back to me and wonder what he'd done to be given away. Then the cycle would continue each time I left and the pet would get more confused each time. No. I won't put an animal through that."

Hannah smiled and clapped her hands. "Great. You don't have an objection to a pet as long as someone else takes care of it, right?"

Joe narrowed his eyes. "What do you have in mind?"

Hannah put her hands behind her back and swayed back and forth. "I thought I'd get a kitten or a puppy. Something to keep me and the baby company when you're off chasing bounties."

Joe cocked his head to one side and lifted an eyebrow. "Are you trying to make me feel guilty?"

"No."

"Because it's working."

Hannah grinned. "Well, maybe…a little, anyway." Her shoulders sagged. "I'll miss you Joe and it hurts that you won't miss me, too."

He furrowed his brows. "Who said I won't miss you?"

She was sad and heartbroken. "How can you miss me if you don't love me?"

"Not feeling love doesn't mean I won't miss you. I care for you a great deal. You're my friend as well as my wife. That makes you pretty darn important to me."

Hannah took a deep breath and held her ground. "Not important enough to retire and raise horses though."

Joe closed his eyes and squeezed the flesh between them. "Hannah, we've been over this problem. You know I have to bring him in. I can't let him get away with murder and with shooting me. You know I can't. You wouldn't let Chester leave me behind because you knew I'd need to avenge myself."

She looked up at him, her eyes filling with tears she was doing her best not to let fall. "I know, but I've changed my mind. I don't want to be alone when I have this baby. I don't want to raise this child by myself."

He stepped forward with his arms open wide.

She stepped back and batted away his arms.

"I won't let you sidetrack me with one of your wonderful hugs or with sweet words that make me forget I'm mad."

"Wonderful hugs, huh?"

"Don't look for a compliment." She couldn't help it. She blinked and the tears flowed down her cheeks. The dam had been broken, the river unleased.

He walked forward.

She held an arm straight out in front of her. "Stay where you are. Don't come closer."

Joe ignored her, wrapped his arms around her and held her.

Feeling him, his body and his scent surrounding her, she sagged in his arms, no longer able or willing to support herself.

He held her up, held her close and kissed the top of her head.

"Everything will be all right. You hear me, love? Everything will be fine. Let's just get you in the wagon so you can lay down for a spell."

Hannah nearly collapsed hearing him call her *love*. She struggled, without any strength behind it. "I can't lie down. I have to help Lydia with our meal. I—"

"You need to lie down," said Lydia from behind Hannah. "I can handle a meal without you, as I've done many times. Joe is taking care of the animals, so you have no excuse not to rest for a little bit. I'll call you when the food is ready."

Hannah looked at the two people she loved most in the world. They were a united front now and they would not take 'no' for an answer.

"All right. I'll lay down. Just for a few minutes. You understand, just for a few minutes."

"We understand." Joe looked over at Lydia and winked. "We understand perfectly."

Lydia smiled and nodded. "Yes. Perfectly."

Hannah closed her eyes and shook her head slowly. "I know you two are up to something, but right now, I am very tired and don't care what you're planning to do with me."

"We *plan* on letting you rest," said Joe. "That's all, rest."

"Fine. Good day." Hannah climbed into the wagon and laid on the pile of blankets and sacks of flour. All in all she was pretty comfortable.

Now if she could just figure out how to get Joe to realize he loves her. He gave himself away when he called her 'love'. Why would he say it if he didn't mean it?

CHAPTER 15

When Hannah awoke, darkness had fallen. She climbed out of the wagon, madder than a wet hornet.

"What in the world were you two thinking? Leaving me to sleep so long. I thought we were supposed to—"

Hannah looked for Joe, turning in a complete circle, before returning her gaze to her sister.

"Where's Joe?"

"Gone."

"Gone? Where?"

"To check out the mountain trail, both up and down. He won't be back until tomorrow night."

"I thought clearing the trail was what we were supposed to do tomorrow...with the wagon."

"We were, but he wanted to make sure we didn't run into any, uh, roadblocks."

"Why would he do that? If there are problems, we need to be there to help him clear them away."

She braced her feet apart and waved her hands. "That's exactly what he said you'd say. He said to tell you that you're expecting and shouldn't be doing heavy lifting or anything like that. He wants you to take it easy and rest until you're feeling better. Joe's worried about you, Hannah."

Hannah shook her head and headed over to the fire where Lydia cooked their meal. "He's worried about the baby. He doesn't love me. Oh, he says he cares for me, and that's all he can give me."

Lydia pointed her finger at her sister. "Don't be an idiot. Of course, he loves you. He doesn't treat anyone else with the kindness he does you. He's always touching you, holding you in his arms, kissing you and not just on your lips. He kisses the top of your head and your neck and…need I go on? You don't see him doing those things to me, and I believe Joe cares for me."

Hannah stopped dead in her tracks. Could it be? Did Joe love her and not realize it, just as she didn't recognize it as love? His love is what she'd prayed for and it appeared her prayers had been answered. Now, if she could just get Joe to realize it, too.

Joe returned the next evening, his steps slow and his shoulders stooped looking dog tired.

Hannah ran to him as he dismounted.

"You look exhausted. Supper is ready and hot. Chester gave us a rabbit and Lydia made a stew with some of the potatoes and carrots we got at South Pass City. Come. Sit. I'll get you a cup of coffee."

"Thanks. I'd rather have a kiss."

Hannah smiled, thinking of what Lydia had said. She was right. Joe did like to kiss her every chance he got.

She walked into his open arms and wrapped her arms around his neck before kissing him with all the love in her heart.

When they pulled apart, Joe smiled. "You must have missed me. That was some kiss."

"I did. I was very mad when I woke up and you were gone, but Lydia explained and you were right. I would have insisted on going, too, and that would not have been good for me."

His eyes widened and he pulled back while still keeping his arms around her. "I can't believe my ears. Say it again."

Her eyebrows furrowed, she asked, "What? What do you want me to say?"

He grinned. "That I was right."

Hannah chuckled. "Fine. No need to gloat. You were right, okay?"

"Ah, come on. Let me enjoy my victory. I don't have them very often."

"I intend to keep it that way. I don't want you to think you get your way every time we disagree."

He raised his hands in front of him. "I definitely know better than to believe that." He pulled her close. "You are my spunky wife, remember? I like that you hold your position when you believe you're right. By the same token, I like that you admit when you're wrong."

Hannah stepped back and picked at her skirt for some nonexistent lint. "Will you admit when you're wrong?"

Joe crossed his arms over his chest. "If I ever am, yes, I'll admit it. You have to show me how I'm wrong and why before I'll make the admission."

She nodded. "You must do the same."

He gave her a single nod. "Fair enough."

Hannah took his hand and led him to the fire.

"Let me get you that coffee."

As soon as he sat, Lydia handed him a plate with a bowl full of stew and two hot biscuits slathered with butter.

"Here you go. There's plenty more where that came from. As it is we'll be having that for breakfast and maybe lunch."

"Even after feeding the animals?" he teased.

Lydia put her hands on her hips. "Yes, even after feeding the animals. They got the carcass and have been very happily gnawing on the bones."

Joe smiled and cocked an eyebrow. "Great. I hate to see good bones go to waste."

Lydia laughed and turned back to the fire. She dished up another plate and handed it to Hannah.

"Here, eat. The horses and oxen can wait."

She hesitated, knowing she should take care of the animals first. "I shouldn't."

Lydia lowered her chin a notch. "The chores aren't going anywhere and if you wait, I'll help, and we'll be done sooner."

"Okay." She took the plate from Lydia and sat next to Joe. "I'm only doing this so I can eat supper with my husband."

He grinned. "Thanks. I like having supper with my wife."

"I don't think I'll ever get used to being called your wife."

"Why not? My wife is what you are."

"I know but I never thought...well, I never thought I'd be married, much less to you." *I never thought I'd be married to the man of my dreams, the one that I love.*

"What do you mean, to me?"

Her heartbeat hastened and she looked at her plate. "I just mean to someone...well...who could have any woman he chooses."

He put his shoulders back and sat up straighter. "Any woman I choose, huh? I chose you. Even before we got caught kissing, I chose you, or don't you remember?"

"I figured you were just being kind, because of

my feet." She lifted one leg and jutted her chin toward the foot. "You know."

"Our friendship might have started that way, but I kept coming around because I liked you and wanted to get to know you." He smiled wide. "I think they call that courting."

"I was too stupid to realize what you were doing."

"Don't call yourself stupid." His brows furrowed and the skin between his eye wrinkled. "Never say that again in my hearing. You are not stupid. You're quite likely one of the smartest women I've ever met…you and Lydia both. I mean, you know Swahili, for goodness sake."

Heat filled Hannah's cheeks. "We just read a couple of articles that's all."

"That's all, you say. How many of these other women do you figure have read the same article or any story about current events?"

"I don't have any idea. What I'd like to know is why haven't you said anything about the trail up ahead?"

Joe let out a long breath. "I was hoping you'd forget about my excursion."

Hannah reached over and touched his knee. "Is the road that bad? Really?"

He shook his head. "For the most part, it's a pretty good road. But about halfway down the other side is a narrow track along a cliff. One wrong move and you'll be over the edge in a matter of seconds."

She gasped and raised her hand to cover her mouth. "Oh, no. What will we do?"

"Nothing to do. We have to go forward and take our chances. We have no choice."

"When do we start?"

Lydia brought her plate and sat. "What are you talking about?"

Hannah pointed at the steep incline ahead. "The trip over the mountains. We'll start it tomorrow, I believe."

Joe swallowed and nodded. "First thing in the morning. I want us on the road at daybreak, which means getting up about four o'clock in the morning. Do you think you can do it?"

Hannah nodded. "We can do it. You'll have to get me up and I'll wake Lydia." She looked over at her sister. "You'll have to feed your pets early. I hope they don't get used to it."

"They'll be fine. I promise."

Four o'clock in the morning was definitely too early for a civilized person to be rising from the bed.

Joe rubbed her arm, waking her gently. "Get up, sweetheart. Time to rise and shine."

She moved closer to him. "I don't want to."

He chuckled. "You never want to get up. I'm gratified that you want to spend more time in bed with me, however, today is special. We have no choice but to get up now." He pulled the blankets off of her. "So get up, darlin'. We have work to do."

Hannah wasn't so asleep that she didn't hear the endearments he spoke. She simply thought she must be dreaming. Joe wouldn't call her those things and yet before, just a few days ago, he'd called her "love". Did he really have those feelings for her now? What changed?

She yawned and got dressed. When she walked outside the tent, it was still dark.

She looked over at Joe who was putting on the coffee. "Are we really leaving before daylight?"

"No, but we are doing our chores and eating breakfast, which Lydia will be preparing after she feeds her pets, in the dark."

Placing her hands at her waist, she stretched her back. "I'll milk the cow."

"I'll round up your walking side of beef after I get this coffee on the fire."

Hannah looked at the flames. "I think you'll need a bigger fire than that."

"No, I won't. We don't want a huge fire, just one big enough for one or two pots. Today, for instance, just the coffee and the stew pot."

"What about the biscuits?"

He shrugged. "We'll have to skip them today, much to my dismay."

"We'll be ready to leave in half an hour. Will that be soon enough?"

"Yes. Does that give you time to eat? No skipping meals for you."

"You worry too much." *I'm happy he cares enough about the baby that he inadvertently cares for me, too. He doesn't realize he's doing it, and I'm not about to tell him.*

They finished eating and packed up in record time. By a quarter before seven, they were traveling up the mountain.

This part doesn't seem so bad, but Joe said the really bad, and I'm assuming really scary, part was on the downside of the Wind River Range.

At the top of the pass, they stopped, rested the animals and ate lunch which was the remaining rabbit stew, coffee, and fresh biscuits. Lydia had put the biscuits together in the wagon on their way uphill, so all she had to do was put the Dutch oven on the hot coals, put some of the coals on the lid and let them bake for about fifteen minutes. The timing was always a little longer out here in the wild than it was at home in an oven.

Lunch was cooked and consumed in about forty minutes, getting them back on the road in less than an hour.

The road down the other side of the mountain was hardly more than an animal path. No, animal trail wasn't true. Hannah could see the wagon tracks from previous trains.

About two hours from when they started down they reached the cliff Joe had told her about.

He stopped, dismounted and walked back to the wagon.

"This is where we change places. You ride the horse and I drive."

"All right." She set the brake and climbed down. "I'll walk the horse so I can be beside Lydia."

"That's fine. A good idea as a matter of fact. The road gets a bit slippery for the horse up ahead because of the loose rock on the trail which is also solid rock at that location."

Hanna and Lydia walked down the mountain trail behind the wagon. The wagon was moving so slow the rest of the wagon train caught them. Some of the wagons were traveling faster than the others. One, in particular, pulled by six mules, started down the mountain. The women, Esther and Ruth Huckabee reached the cliff just as Joe, Hannah, and Lydia had finished crossing the treacherous terrain.

Hannah and Lydia waved their hands and shouted for the wagon to slow down. But it didn't hitting the cliff way too fast.

Hannah turned and watched as the mules slid on the rock, desperately searching for purchase. She saw the fright on the faces of the two women that until that point had been grinning; obviously pleased they were making such good time.

She heard their screams as they fell off the cliff and into the ravine below.

She buried her face in Joe's shirt. Then she, Joe, and Lydia looked over the side and saw the wagon in a million pieces. The mules weren't moving.

Tears ran down Lydia's cheeks. "No one could have survived that."

Hannah turned her face back into Joe's chest, tears wetting his coat. He put his arms around her and shook his head. "Probably not, but we'll check when we get to the bottom. If they didn't survive they'll need to be buried."

Hannah pulled back and sniffled. "If they did survive, they'll need to be tended to for the rest of the journey."

"I know if it were me," said Lydia. "I wouldn't want to survive if it meant being like a vegetable for life. I don't want to be a burden on anyone."

"I agree with that sentiment." Joe looked at Hannah. "Please don't make me live in that condition."

She cupped his face. "I'll do that for you and expect you to do the same for me."

Once again he leaned into her hand, but this time instead of pulling away he covered her hand with his. Then he turned his head and kissed her palm.

Hannah didn't know what to think or what to do. Did these little shows of affection mean he loved her? Was he just being kind because of the baby? No, he'd always been kind. Heavens when they first met he helped her clean her bloody feet and then bandaged them.

What was she supposed to do...to think? How was she supposed to act? What if she acted the way she felt? Would he still act loving toward her?

CHAPTER 16

The remainder of the wagons made it safely down the cliff and the rest of the way to the bottom of the mountain.

Joe, Chester Gunn, Hannah and two more of the men working the wagon train, went up the ravine to the scene of the accident. Everyone was dead, including the mules and for that she thanked God. No one would want to live in the condition they would have been in.

Hannah prepared the bodies for burial.

The men dug two holes deep enough that animals couldn't dig them up.

The Huckabee sisters were originally from Louisville, Kentucky. They'd both answered ads from men in Oregon City and were headed there to find a new life. Now someone, probably Reverend

Trowbridge, would have to tell their prospective husbands they were gone.

Joe came up to her and laid a hand on her shoulder.

She reached up and clasped his hand, appreciative of his strength. Days like today didn't make her feel good about the trek she was on and in fact, she questioned the trip as a whole.

Hannah was the only woman on the train who had achieved her dreams. She'd married Joe, not in the way she'd wanted to, but the deed was done and now they were expecting their first child. *The first of many.* These two poor women had died trying to better themselves.

Joe wrapped his arms around her.

"I'm sorry. We probably shouldn't have had you prepare them to be buried."

"I'm fine."

He wiped her cheek with his thumb.

When she looked at his hand and saw the glitter of liquid on his thumb, she realized she was crying.

"I'm sorry." She wiped her face with her palms. "They had so much to look forward to—new husbands, new families, new lives. Why would they risk it as they did? They knew not to drive the mules so fast. What did they think they would prove, except how not to drive down this trail?"

"I don't know. But what I do know is everyone else paid attention when I told them to go as slow

210

as possible. They let us use the ropes to keep the wagons from moving faster than the animals could go. No one else tried to show off."

"Do you really think that is what they were doing? Showing off?"

"I don't have any other reason for their actions. If I'm not mistaken, those animals were racing mules. Perhaps they simply couldn't control them."

"I'd like to believe their death wasn't their fault, but I can't. I saw their faces. Their smiles were full of glee. They wanted the thrill of racing down the mountain."

"I know. I saw them, too."

"Well, I've cleaned and prepared them as well as I could. They are ready for burial."

The service was somber, as you would expect for a funeral, but the tenseness remained even after they were buried and everyone had returned to their wagons. Everyone spoke in whispers, as though afraid to invoke the wrath of the Gods.

None of the supplies in the wagon was salvageable, destroyed when the wagon hit the valley floor. The mules would provide meat for the rest of the trip for those that needed it. Lydia took some for her babies. The rest was left to the scavengers.

The atmosphere at her wagon was somber. None of them seemed to have anything to say. They ate in silence, cleaned up and went to bed in the quiet.

Hannah went without her nightgown. She wanted to feel Joe's body with his skin warming her.

Joe seemed to know what she needed. He held her, kissed her, pulled her body on top of him and made love to her. All in silence. Even when they reached the pinnacle of their lovemaking, they were quiet, kissing, swallowing the sound coming from the other. Living next to Lydia, they'd learned how to make love quietly.

After both were replete, Joe tucked her into his side and they fell asleep.

Hannah dreamed of the accident.

Joe woke her.

Her screams must have awakened him.

She shook, fear gripping her as she clutched the quilts.

Lydia called from outside the tent. "Hannah! Are you all right? Joe?"

Joe squeezed Hannah's shoulders. "She's fine, Lydia. Just a bad dream."

Hannah heard the concern in her sister's voice. "I'm okay, Lydie. I just relived today in my sleep."

"All right. I'll go back to bed but I'm here if you need me."

"Thank you. I love you, Lydie."

"I love you, too, big sister."

"Goodnight, Lydia," said Joe.

"Goodnight, Joe. Call me if she has anymore... dreams. We might just as well get up, have some tea and sit around the fire for a while before trying to sleep again."

"I'll keep it in mind," said Joe.

Hannah heard her walk back to the wagon and climb inside. Her pets slept with her whether in the tent or in the wagon or under the stars.

Joe pulled Hannah close, wrapping both of his arms around her. "How are you?"

With her head on Joe's shoulder, she still shook and couldn't seem to get warm, no matter how close she got to him. "I'll be okay. I saw the accident, only I was the one going off the cliff. My dream scared the you-know-what out of me."

"I heard you, but I'm here. I won't let anything happen to you. Do you understand?"

"Yes." She snuggled into him, willing his warmth to inhabit her and chase away the cold. *Do I understand? Is he trying to tell me he loves me? Or is that really me seeing what I want?*

The next morning they pulled out away from the Wind River Range and headed west again across the high prairie. At Fort Hall, they stopped for supplies and then forged on, following the Snake River to the Blue Mountains.

These mountains were the last obstacle they would have to cross before finally traveling west to the Willamette Valley and Oregon City. The range was formidable, but no one raced down these mountains.

Joe insisted they cross just as they had the Wind River Range with him driving the wagon and she and Lydia following with the horses and livestock.

The trek was slow going, but the way was not as dangerous as the Wind River Range. Everyone arrived at the bottom of the mountain safe and sound.

As the last wagon came down, everyone shouted with joy.

Hannah looked around. Everyone gathered to watch the last wagon come down. Then she heard "Joe! Joe! Joe!" They cheered her husband, as well they should. If not for him leading the way, they would have lost many more people, animals, and wagons.

She joined in the cheer. "Joe! Joe! Joe!"

He turned beet red.

Hannah took pity on her husband and walked over and raised her arms then brought them down, again, and again to quiet the people. Finally, the crowd stopped cheering and dispersed.

Hannah put an arm around Joe's waist. "They're proud of you and thankful. You brought them through a harrowing experience, not once but twice. They want you to know they appreciate it. I just want you to know I'm proud of you. Proud to call you husband."

He shrugged. "I did my job, that's all."

She smiled. "And we're thankful, that's all."

He finally grinned and shook his head.

"Come on. Let's get going to The Dalles. We can restock what supplies we'll need until you get set up in Oregon City. After The Dalles, we'll travel a ways then take the Barlow Toll Road across the Columbia River. The route is much safer to go around Mt. Hood, rather than down the Columbia on rafts."

She widened her eyes. "Good gracious, I should hope so. How much longer does the trip take?"

"Probably about two weeks, but the road is so much safer, and the toll is cheaper than buying a raft from the Indians. The fee is five dollars for the wagon and ten cents per head for the livestock."

"That still takes a lot of the money we have left."

"I got paid for Jones, remember. I'll pay the tolls. You and Lydia are my family now."

"I know, but I'm not used to pooling money. It's been just me and Lydia for so long, getting used to something else is hard."

"We have time."

The reality of her situation suddenly hit her like a ton of bricks. "We *don't* have time. You'll be leaving as soon as we get settled with Mr. Mosley. I don't know when you'll return or if you'll return. Isn't that about right?"

Joe closed his eyes.

She knew she was right and the situation saddened her. He couldn't deny he was about to abandon his pregnant wife to chase the man who shot him.

She watched him. His eyebrows furled together. Was he angry at her for pointing out what would happen, or at himself for making the incident happen?

He turned his pain-filled gaze on her. "I have to. You know that, have known it all along."

"That doesn't mean I like it." She crossed her arms over her bosom. "I don't. I don't like it at all. With the way my luck is, I'll have the baby before you even find Mr. Smith. I guess what the choice comes down to is what is more important to you getting revenge or your family?"

He shook a fist in the air. "Dammit! It's not that simple."

"Isn't it?"

She trained her gaze on him and didn't blink. Then, when he didn't answer, she turned away and walked over to the wagon where Lydia stood. She kept her back to Joe. She didn't want him to see her cry.

The rest of the trip to Oregon City, Joe slept at Chester's camp. He ate with Chester and the other men working the wagon train. He tried not to check on Hannah, but couldn't help seeing her while he worked. Nor could he stop watching from a distance to make sure Hannah was safe when she went to the river for water.

He kept asking himself if this one last bounty was worth putting his marriage in jeopardy. Why was the bounty so important? Two reasons were evident—Smith shot him and the man killed his own family for another woman. He couldn't let that crime go unpunished and Hannah needed to realize that.

The problem was, as he saw it, Hannah didn't want to be left behind. He understood but the journey was too dangerous and too hard for her to go, especially with her expecting.

He thought of a third option. He could give the information he had to the sheriff at Oregon City and let him deal with it. By his calculations, Smith might have actually come west as far as Oregon City. He'd been heading west, first with the wagon train and then on his own. He could have hooked up with another wagon train or even be following this one at a distance.

Finding a way to keep doing what he was doing and still have Hannah wasn't working. He realized he loved her—her stubbornness, her spirit, her laugh, her beauty which she didn't see. In this moment of clarity he knew one thing. He'd rather die than lose her. He needed to tell her now. See if he could salvage his marriage and keep the woman who meant more to him than anyone, by his side.

The time was nearly dusk and the wagon train

had stopped for the evening. They would reach Oregon City by tomorrow night. He wanted Hannah to know before then, that he loved her. Now was the time she and Malena Farrow usually got water from the river. He headed first to the wagon.

"Lydia, where is Hannah."

"Did you finally come to your senses, Joe Stanton? If you haven't, then leave her be. She's cried enough over you."

Joe walked to Lydia, hugged her and then stepped back.

"I've definitely come to my senses. I can't lose her. I love her, Lydia. Where is she?"

"Down by the river, where she is this time every night, as you're well aware. What are you doing, Joe? Nervous?"

Joe sighed. "Yes, more than I've ever been. What if she doesn't want me back?"

"Go to the river and find out. Standing here talking to me won't help you any."

Joe nodded. Removed his hat and ran his fingers through his hair. "Okay. I'm going."

Joe left the wagon and was about halfway to the river when he heard screams.

Hannah!

He ran as fast as his feet would take him. When he emerged from the trees, he saw Hannah struggling with a man. Smith. Malena Farrow lay on the ground apparently unconscious.

Joe drew his weapon and called out. "Smith. Leave my wife alone."

Hannah looked up and though he knew she was afraid, she managed to smile.

Smith grabbed her by the arm and held his gun to her back.

"Stay away, Stanton. Or I'll kill her. You know I will. I'm already bound to hang. I can't let you take me back."

Suddenly Smith pushed Hannah to the ground and aimed his gun at Joe.

Joe's gun was already out and he lodged three bullets in Smiths body without him even getting off one shot.

"Joe!" Hannah called.

"Hannah."

She was still on the ground.

"What's the matter, love? Are you hurt?"

"I think I sprained my ankle when he pushed me down. Go check Malena. He ambushed us. Malena carries a derringer but he knocked her out before she could get off a shot."

Joe checked Malena who was coming around.

"You all right?"

"Yeah, I'm fine. I'll have a splitting headache for a while," said Malena.

"I'm taking Hannah back to the wagon," said Joe. "She's sprained her ankle."

"Go. I'm fine, really," said Malena.

Joe picked Hannah up in his arms and started back to the wagon train.

She put her arms around his neck.

"I was coming to tell you. I love you, Hannah Stanton. I'm not leaving. Even if Smith hadn't shown up here tonight, I was on my way to find you and tell you I'm staying. You and this baby are more important to me than anything. You are my world."

"Ah, Joe." She rested her head on his shoulder.

He felt the little breaths she took as she cried and was relieved to have made his admission.

Hannah pulled back and looked up at him. "I was going to tell you to go ahead and go, that we'd be here when you got back. I don't want to lose you. I love you. I've loved you, forever. I think since you helped me with my feet that first night. You were so kind and careful not to hurt me. And when you took off your hat and I saw your face, I nearly fainted, you're so handsome. I knew I never had a chance with you. You had a wagon train of women to choose from and any one of them would have chosen you over the unseen man they were supposed to marry. I knew you'd never choose me—"

He grinned. "You're rambling. I love you and you love me. Our love is all that matters."

Hannah nodded and laid her head against his chest. "Yes, that's all that matters."

He carried her back to the wagon.

Lydia looked up from where she stirred a pot over the fire.

"Hannah. What happened? I heard gunshots. Are you wounded?"

"Yes, but not by a bullet. Smith knocked me down and I think I sprained my ankle."

"Here," Lydia pointed at a chair she'd untied from the wagon. "Sit while I get the bandages.

Hannah looked at the chair and back at her sister. "Since when do we use the chairs?"

"Since now. We're getting into Oregon City tomorrow. I want to have our last night on the trail be a comfortable one. Now, sit."

Joe sat on the chair and kept Hannah in his arms.

Lydia frowned and put her hands on her hips. "I meant for her to sit in the chair, Joe. Not you."

"I know what you meant, but I'm not letting her out of my arms." He looked down at Hannah. "I almost lost you, today," he said softly. "In more ways than one. I don't ever want to feel that way again. You're mine, Hannah Stanton, until death do us part, and even then I won't leave your side."

Hannah reached up and caressed his cheek. "I will never let you go. Wherever you go, so do we." She moved her hand to her stomach. "We'll never let you go."

Joe took her lips with his. She seared him to his soul.

"Tell me you love me."

She smiled. "I love you, Joe Stanton. With all my heart."

"Yes, yes, you love each other. Took you long enough to say the words." Lydia got another chair and sat in front of Joe and Hannah. "Now let me bind your ankle and make sure it's not broken." Lydia pressed on the hurt appendage. "It's not broken, I don't think it's even badly sprained. It will probably hurt a couple of days, but if you ride in the back of the wagon and keep it elevated. You'll be fine."

"Great a night in the wagon on lumpy sacks of food."

Joe grinned. "I'll be with you. You can sleep on me. I'm soft."

Hannah laughed. "You're not soft anywhere and that's the way I like it. But I will take you up on your offer. I'd much rather sleep on you than without you any day."

Hannah leaned back and Joe covered her lips with his, while Lydia wrapped Hannah's ankle tightly.

"There. Since you have Joe, you don't have need for crutches, though we can probably make some if you want."

Joe stood with Hannah in his arms. "Don't bother. I'll take her wherever she wants to go and right now that is into the wagon."

Hannah turned in Joe's arms so she could see Lydia. "Do we have any willow bark tea left?"

"Yes, I'll bring you a cup. That will help with the pain."

"You're a good sister to me, Lydie. How can I ever repay you?"

"I'm the one who should be repaying you. I'd have been alone if not for you and I can't stand the thought of being alone."

"That's another reason Joe and I are staying in Oregon City, well, probably outside the city because we want to raise horses and that takes land."

"That sounds wonderful. Let me get the tea. You should be right as rain in a couple of days."

"I already feel better having it bound."

"Good, very good," said Joe. "I don't like seeing you in pain. It makes me hurt in sympathy."

"Oh, sweetie, what will you do when we start having babies?"

"We'll just have to see what happens then."

"Well, you have about seven months to get over it."

EPILOGUE

June, 1863

Hannah stood in the kitchen at the stove taking the last of their supper out of the oven. "Joey, run and tell your father, supper is ready." The nine-year-old boy ran out of the house.

Hannah smiled. He was so much like his father, with his black hair and blue eyes. But he wasn't the only one. All of her children took after their father.

She smoothed a hand over her swollen belly.

"I wonder who you will look like little one. Are you another daddy's baby?"

"Mama, you're talking to your stomach again," admonished Letty, her seven-year-old daughter.

"Just like I talked to you before you were born. I want your baby brother, or sister, to know how very much we all love him or her, even before they are here for us to hug and kiss."

"Mama, kiss me, too."

Mary, her youngest at three, would be the most difficult when the new baby came. She was used to being the baby and having all that attention. Now she'd have to share.

Hannah picked up her daughter, kissed both cheeks and nuzzled her neck.

Mary shrieked and laughed. "Stop, Mama."

Hannah chuckled and put the child on the floor.

"What is all this mirth coming from the kitchen? I could hear it all the way down the street."

Joe walked in the kitchen door and took off his hat and gun belt, hanging both on pegs along the wall by the door. His gun was on a special peg high above the door, where his children could not reach it.

"Daddy!" Mary squealed and ran at her father.

He caught her and lifted her high into the air.

"Daddy," shouted Letty. She hurried across the kitchen to hug her father.

"You would think you kids hadn't seen me all day."

Letty's shout made Hannah smile. She was her studious child and the only time she got excited was seeing her father walk through the door.

As always he took off his badge and gave it to her.

She took it to her parent's bedroom and set it on the bureau.

When she came back, she tugged on her father's arm.

"What do you need, Letty girl?"

"I think Mama is gonna have the baby today."

Joe eyed Hannah and raised one dark brow.

"Why would you think that?"

"Because Mama's been having pains all day today, but she tried to hide them from us kids."

Hannah couldn't believe she'd been found out. Her Letty was more astute than Hannah knew.

Joe stroked his chin.

"Is that true, my sweet wife?"

She relaxed her posture and put her hand on her lower back. "Yes, but I don't know how she knew. I've been very careful not to show when I'm in pain."

"I know," said Letty. "You acted the same way when Mary was born."

"How do you remember something that happened three years ago?" asked Hannah. "You were only four when she was born."

Letty put her hands behind her back and swayed back and forth. "I know but I remember lots of things, almost everything. I just have a really, really good memory that's all."

Joe narrowed his eyes. "Well, wife, are you having this baby tonight?"

"Yes, I probably am, since my water broke about an hour ago."

Joe walked over to Hannah, bent and scooped her into his arms.

"No, Joe we have to feed the children."

"Has supper finished cooking?"

She blinked a few times. "Well, yes, but what does cooking have to do with it."

"If the food is done, they can serve themselves." He turned back to the children, "I'm taking your mama upstairs and putting her to bed. Joey, I expect you to serve your suppers yourselves. Don't give Mary a lot. She hasn't been eating much at night."

As a pain hit, Hannah gritted her teeth.

"I felt your whole body tense. Did you just have a contraction?"

She nodded. "They are getting closer and closer together. It's probably time to send for the doctor."

"After I get you settled in bed, I'll send Joey for Doc. He'll probably be done eating by then." He shook his head. "I swear that kid eats like it's the last meal he'll ever get."

Hannah chuckled as Joe set her feet on the floor.

"You take off your clothes and I'll get the bed ready."

She discarded her garments and donned a plain cotton nightgown.

Joe pulled back all the covers including the bottom sheet. On the mattress, he laid a huge oilcloth that covered nearly the whole bed. Then he put the sheets back on.

"Okay. The bed is all ready for you and our newest child."

Hannah laid down, her back relaxed, and when the next contraction came, she let the pain roll through her like a wave in the ocean.

"I'm sending Joey for the doctor now. He can finish eating when he comes back."

Joe left the room and returned shortly.

"He's gone. They should be back in about fifteen or twenty minutes. Can you hold off until then?"

"What am I supposed to say to the baby? Hold on, the doctor's not here."

Joe chuckled.

She frowned. "Don't you dare laugh at me."

He opened his eyes wide. "Who me? I would never laugh at you. Just at the situation, we find ourselves in."

She nodded and smiled. And then she chuckled. Then she moaned as another pain hit her.

Joe sat next to her on the bed. "How are you doing, darlin'? Can I do anything for you? Do you want me to hold you?"

"Yes, please."

"Whatever you need."

He scooted up, rested his back on the headboard and gathered her in his arms.

"Holding you like this brings back memories."

"Yes, I've made the same request of you with each of our babies."

"So you have. I like this. I like holding you

especially when you have our new son or daughter in your arms."

A knock sounded on their bedroom door and the doctor appeared. He was a young man, about forty, the same age as Joe. His blond hair was cut short and he abstained from any facial hair. He had interesting green eyes. They were the color of fresh summer lettuce with a black ring around the iris.

"I always find you two like this. How are you, Hannah?"

"I'm good, Doc."

The doctor washed his hands in the basin with the soap and water Hannah put there for him before she prepared supper.

"All right. Joe, I need for you to leave and send Lydia upstairs, please. She's waiting for the word."

"Okay, Doc, but you know I'll be back." Joe leaned down and kissed Hannah on the forehead. "See you soon, my love."

She was tired and excited. "I'm not going anywhere."

Joe chuckled and gave her another kiss.

"Now that he's gone and I don't have to put on the brave face, *get this baby out of me*."

The doctor stood near the end of the bed, drying his hands with a towel. "In his own good time, Hannah. You know that."

"I know Doc, but I've been having pains all day. I didn't want to get you until I was sure the time was close."

"All right. Let's have a look."

Hannah lay back and raised her knees opening them wide so the doctor could see if the baby was coming.

The door opened and Lydia hurried over to the bed.

She took Hannah's hand and quickly squeezed it. "Hi, big sister, how are you?"

"Ready for this to be over."

"I know how you feel. It will be over soon."

"Distract me, Lydie. Tell me about your latest pets."

Lydia slumped a little. "Well, we had some sad tidings. We lost Simba two days ago. He was over ten years old, so he had a long life and we gave him a good one. He always thought he was a housecat and wanted to sit on my lap. We compromised and he sat next to me on the sofa."

"I'm sorry for your loss."

"If you two ladies are through visiting I think we could deliver a baby here soon," said Doc Bishop.

"I'm ready," said Hannah.

"Yes, you are. I want you to push now. Lydia let her squeeze your hands."

Lydia's eyes widened. "You don't know what you're asking. She'll break my hands."

"She won't break mine," said Joe from the doorway.

Doc Bishop looked over at Joe, rolled his eyes and shook his head.

"Every year you find a reason to be in here when Hannah gives birth. I suppose next time I should just let you stay."

"I tried Doc. I went downstairs to be with the kids, and I paced back and forth, back and forth. My son finally stopped me and said "go be with Mama". So here I am. And it looks like my services are needed."

"Yes, yes." The doctor waved at him. "Make yourself useful and hold her hands. Hannah, you push when I say."

Hannah looked up at Joe and smiled at her handsome husband. After all these years she still felt like the luckiest woman in the world that he'd picked her. Her heart was so full it was near to bursting with happiness.

He gave her a watery smile.

"You always get choked up when we have another child."

"I know. I just remember how close I came to losing you."

"Push. Come on now, push!" said Doc.

Hannah bore down as hard as she could. She knew how to do it by now and she squeezed Joe's hands as tight as she could. When she couldn't push anymore, she stopped and rested.

Push and rest, push and rest. Again and again. She did that for what seemed like hours, but she hoped was only about thirty minutes or so.

"Come on now," said Doc. "Give me your biggest push ever. Let's get this little one out to meet you."

She knew the head was out, and now she felt the baby slide from her body and was relieved the baby was finally here.

A small cry echoed throughout the room.

"Well, looks like you have a little boy this time. Two of each," said Doc.

She watched him hand her son to his aunt. He was so small and she wanted him in her arms so much they ached.

"Lydia will get him all cleaned up. You and I still have to deliver the afterbirth. I don't want you to have any complications."

After the doctor finished with her, he washed his hands again. He walked over to his doctor's bag, drying his hands as he went.

"You are amazing. Hannah, you were built to have children," said Doc.

"I don't know about that, Doc. But I'm happy this one is here and I don't have to push anymore."

Lydia came over then, beaming and holding the new baby.

"Here you go, little man. Here's your mama."

The baby fussed.

"Hi, there sweetheart. Remember me? It's Mama." She opened the loose swaddling. "Look he's got my hair. Finally, one of my children who actually looks like me."

The baby quieted and opened his eyes wide.

Joe chuckled. He reached down and put a finger in the baby's hand.

The baby wrapped his tiny fingers around his father's.

Hannah knew Joe always loved when his babies grasped his finger like they are saying "I love you".

She stared at her son, taking in every little face he made. Some that looked like smiles, definite frowns, and so many others. "He's so perfect. Look at him, Joe. Isn't he the most beautiful baby?"

"All of our children are beautiful."

Hannah couldn't take her eyes from her son. "What will we name him? We only have girl's names decided since we were sure we'd have a girl again."

Joe tickled the little one's belly. "I don't know. What about your father? What was his name?"

"Raymond." Just the name brought her so many wonderful memories of her, Lydie and their parents together. Her eyes misted.

"Ray Stanton. I like it. What do you think?"

"Dad's full name was Raymond Noah Granger. We'll call him Raymond Noah Stanton."

"Sounds good. What do you think, Lydie? Should we name him after Dad?"

"I think that's great. Dad would be pleased."

Hannah noticed Lydie was tearing up, too.

"When do you want the kids up here?" Lydie dabbed at her eyes with a hanky.

233

"Not until after I nurse him. Say in about thirty minutes."

"Okay, I'll go down and stay with them until then."

"Thanks, Lydie."

The doctor closed his bag and smiled at Hannah and her family. "Well, you don't need me anymore. I'll be back in a couple of days to make sure everything is going well."

"Thanks, Doc," said Joe. "What do I owe you for this one?"

"Well, sheriff, two dollars ought to cover it."

Joe pulled out his wallet and dug out two dollar bills.

"Thanks again, Doc," said Hannah.

"You two are my favorite patients. I don't have to sew you up with a bullet wound and you give me lots of babies to deliver."

At the mention of bullet wounds, Joe and Hannah both chuckled. No one except Lydia and the previous sheriff, knew what Joe used to do for a living. He'd had to let the ex-sheriff, Robert McCauley, know before he hired him as a deputy. Then when Robert quit and decided to go south to try his luck in the gold fields Joe became the sheriff of Oregon City.

He still had some excitement but not nearly as much danger and he was home every night for dinner and to play with his kids.

Hannah loved that about her husband. He really enjoyed his children. From fishing to reading to riding horses, he included them all when they were old enough—the boys and the girls.

She looked up at him. His mouth was turned up in a smile and his eyes, those dark blue pools gazed back. Then his mouth was on hers, kissing her and loving her.

When they parted, Hannah reached up and caressed his cheek. "I love you. From the moment you carried me into the stream to take care of my feet, I've been yours."

"And you, my sweet, stubborn wife, I love you. You've given me all that I need and all that I never knew I wanted. You and my kids. You mean everything to me."

The baby started to fuss again.

His little cries were more squeaks than anything else, but they caused her breasts to feel full, ready for him to nurse.

She opened her gown and after a bit of prodding and teasing, he finally latched on and suckled.

Joe stayed, as he always did, while the baby nursed. The first time was always just the three of them—bonding, learning, loving.

This family was the pot of gold at the end of the rainbow. The home at the end of a two thousand mile journey.

This had to be heaven because life couldn't get any sweeter.

ABOUT THE AUTHOR

CYNTHIA WOOLF is the award winning and best-selling author of twenty-five historical western romance books and two short stories with more books on the way.

Cynthia loves writing and reading romance. Her first western romance, *Tame A Wild Heart*, was inspired by the story her mother told her of meeting Cynthia's father on a ranch in Creede, Colorado. Although *Tame A Wild Heart* takes place in Creede that is the only similarity between the stories. Her father was a cowboy not a bounty hunter and her mother was a nursemaid (called a nanny now) not the ranch owner. The ranch they met on is still there as part of the open space in Mineral County in southwestern Colorado.

Writing as CA Woolf, she has six sci-fi, space opera romance titles. She calls them westerns in space.

Cynthia credits her wonderfully supportive husband Jim and her critique partners for saving her sanity and allowing her to explore her creativity.

WEBSITE
http://cynthiawoolf.com

NEWSLETTER
https://www.subscribepage.com/k1p2m1